Also by E.P. Garth

Off the Air: A Pat Cassidy Novel

Out of Touch

#2. 3/13/11 Started.

A Pat Cassidy Novel

Copyright © 2010 E.P. Garth

ISBN 978-1-60910-287-6

All rights reserved. No part of this publication may be reproduced, stored in a retrieval system, or transmitted in any form or by any means, electronic, mechanical, recording or otherwise, without the prior written permission of the author.

Printed in the United States of America.

The characters and events in this book are fictitious. Any similarity to real persons, living or dead, is coincidental and not intended by the author.

Booklocker.com, Inc. 2010

Author's website: http://epgarthlearn.com
Publisher's website: http://www.booklocker.com

Acknowledgments

The writing process, at least for me, is like the ancient African adage, "It takes an entire village to raise a child." Without the support and willingness of others to help in this venture there would have never been a first book, much less a second. Foremost in this effort has been my wife, Sue, who with encouragement and dogged determination has helped me write both OFF THE AIR and OUT OF TOUCH. During the editing process she has taken the lead to tirelessly read and re-read the manuscripts and to involve others in order to receive an outside perspective. In doing so, we have gotten invaluable input from both our daughters, Amanda and Kimberly, my mother and father in-law, Madeline and O.Q. Quick, and sister-in-law, Judy Quick. My cousin, Kevin Graves, has done such a masterful job designing both book covers.

Particularly during the writing of OUT OF TOUCH, I have been given a lot of advice from my brother and sister in-law, Richard and Pam Quick. They helped me capture the ambiance of San Miguel de Allende, Mexico through countless emails and pictures from their time spent in that beautiful city.

I would also like to thank Teresa McAnally for her description of Waterloo Park in Austin, Texas, and Janet Elam for helping me remember how the IBM typewriters worked in the 1970s.

In memory of my inspiration, Robert B. Parker 1932-2010

For Brady and Bailey

Who give me new reasons to write

*Frankie,
Thanks for buying my books. Enjoy! E.P. Garth*

Out of Touch

E.P. Garth

Chapter One

Sheriff Glenn Vogel sat behind his desk in the Brown County Sheriff's Department looking down at the hat he was holding in his lap. I sat in front of his desk watching his face as he attempted to regain his composure. Behind him was a mahogany gun case with six rifles locked behind the glass door. Three shotguns, two thirty-thirties, and a thirty-aught-six. Hanging on the wall to the right of the gun case was a large shadow box with nine different strands of barbed-wire. Each strand has a different name. And each has a different story.

The Sheriff looked up at me and took a deep breath.

"It's hard for me to talk about Kerry," Vogel said.

"What kind of kid was he?" I said.

"The pride of my life is what he was. No father could have been any prouder of a son than I was of Kerry. Popular with the girls, his classmates, and the best quarterback Brownwood, Texas, had ever seen."

"I know about all that," I said, "but what kind of person was he?"

"Like a lot of kids back then. Fun loving, not thinking much about how precious youth is, living from day to day."

"Kid's are like that even today," I said.

"Times never really change, do they, Pat?"

"No, they don't."

Sheriff Vogel looked away and gazed around the room and began to smile.

"You know, I thought when he went off to Austin to play football he would end up in professional football someday. Kerry was that good."

"Why did he choose Texas?" I said.

"Cause they're Texas mainly, but he liked Mike Earl."

"That would be Darrell King's assistant?"

"Yeah, he recruits this area and Kerry thought the world of him. Mike spent so much time with us he became like a part of the family."

"Isn't that illegal according to NCAA rules?"

"Hell, I don't know," he said. "Back then I don't think so, but these days, maybe. Ain't kept up with college ball since Kerry disappeared."

"I suppose Kerry liked to party?" I asked.

"Yeah," Vogel said. "I told him the smokin' and drinkin' would hurt him on the football field someday, but he never paid any attention to me because he was so much better than everyone else."

"Did he use drugs?"

"You tell me, Pat. Kerry's about your age. What were you doing in 1968?"

"I was in Vietnam," I said, "but I saw my share of drugs."

"Ever get into that stuff?" Vogel said.

"No," I said. "I was lucky in that respect."

"Luck had nothing to do with it. You just made the right choice…Kerry didn't."

"What kind of drugs did he use?"

"He smoked marijuana," Vogel said, "but that was all I knew about."

"Sometimes that's all it takes," I said.

"Back then," Vogel said, "we didn't have much of a drug problem around here. A little marijuana got into the county, but it wasn't anything we had to deal with on a daily basis. Not anything like now."

Vogel put his hat on the desk, shifted in his chair and crossed his legs. The creases in his khaki uniform were sharp and straight at the sleeves and trousers. The collar was open at the neck and he wore a white t-shirt underneath. His silver badge gleamed under the fluorescent lights and his holster carried a Smith and Wesson .38 with a strap snapped over the hammer.

"What do you think happened?" I said.

Vogel looked me in the eyes and inhaled air slowly and then blew the air out through his mouth.

"I wish I knew," he said. "After eight months of searching I could never come to a conclusion whether he was dead or alive."

"What's your gut feeling tell you?"

"He's dead," he said. "But ask me tomorrow and I'll have a different answer for you."

"Where did you lose his trail?" I said.

"In Austin," Vogel said. "Kerry just vanished."

"What did they tell you at UT?"

"Coach Earl said as far as he knew everything was fine. Kerry was late for practice a couple of times and seemed to be a little preoccupied with something other than football, but he didn't believe it was a red herring."

"Given much thought to what might have been bothering him?"

"Yeah, a lot," he said.

"Come up with anything?"

"No, the semester hadn't even started yet. The team was still in two-a-days."

"Girlfriends?" I said.

"Sure, but no attachments."

"How about in Austin?"

"He had only been there a month, but the best I could tell he wasn't seeing anyone."

The phone buzzed and Vogel picked up the receiver. He listened to the voice at the other end of the line. I could hear a female voice but couldn't make out what she was saying.

"That'll be all right," he said. "Tell Mac to take care of it before he leaves, and Annie, bring me a cup of coffee."

Vogel looked at me. "You wanna cup, Pat?"

"Love a cup. Black."

A few minutes later Annie brought a couple of coffee mugs into Vogel's office and sat them down in front of us. *Annie's uniform fits her better than the sheriff's.*

"Annie, you remember Pat Cassidy don't you?"

"How could I forget?" Annie said.

She smiled and left the room.

"Nice girl that Annie," Vogel said. "She went to high school with my son."

"Pretty girl," I said.

"Yeah, we're lucky to have her."

"Any skeletons in your closet that I should know about, Sheriff?"

"Other than the fact I was wild as a March hair when I was young?"

"Yes, other than that," I said.

"Nothing that would make Kerry want to disappear and never come back home."

"Was he rebellious?" I said.

"Not really. You know, Pat, we raised him right, his mother and me. Always went to church on Sundays when he was growing up, were involved in all his school activities, monitored the people he hung around with the best we could until he started driving. Kerry was well rounded and had such a great future in front of him."

I sipped some of the coffee while it was still hot. The Sheriff picked up his cup and moved it off his desk calendar onto a yellow notepad.

"What if we find out he's dead?" I said.

"Then his mother and me will finally be able to bury'em and put his life into perspective."

"What if he's alive?"

"Then his mother and me want to see him."

"What if he doesn't want to see you?"

"Why wouldn't he?"

"Don't know, but what *if* that's what *he* wants?"

"I don't know," he said, "but let's cross that bridge when we get to it. You haven't found him yet."

"I will, though."

"You sound pretty sure of yourself," Vogel said. "What makes you so sure you're going to find him eight years after the fact and a cold trail?"

"Something just tells me we're going to find him."

Chapter Two

Last time I left the Brown County Sheriff Department it was through the back door at the stroke of midnight during a jailbreak. It wasn't much of jailbreak. Jeb Glasscock, my boss, slipped me a key and I simply walked out of the building while the deputy sheriff on duty slept at the front desk. Now, less than a month later, April was in full bloom as I stopped on the sidewalk in front of the nineteenth century jail. The new Brown County Jail around the corner was scheduled to open in November. The pecan and live oak trees that lined the street were budding out and the peach tree blossoms were fragrant in the backyard of a home cattycorner across the street. It was a quiet and pleasant morning in Brownwood, so I decided to walk to the Club Café two blocks away where I was to have breakfast with Deputy Sheriff J.T. Lambert. When I arrived at the restaurant, he was standing at the counter in front of the cash register talking to a man dressed in a short sleeve white shirt with a brown clip-on tie.

"Hey, Pat," J.T. said as I walked through the front door. "Want you to meet Dale Wilson, the owner."

Wilson reached out with his large right hand and as we shook hands, he smiled more with his eyes than any other part of his face. In the right circles he could have been passed off as a football coach with his strong physical makeup. J.T. stood tall and erect in his uniform that bristled with authority. The .44 Magnum strapped to his hip and his silver badge reflected the brightness of the early morning sun flooding in through the front door and windows.

"Let's sit over here, Pat," J.T. said, pointing at the front booth.

He placed his straw Stetson in the seat next to him. I settled in the seat across from him and picked up the breakfast menu.

"I'll be free this time next week," J.T. said. "Sheriff hired a deputy from Erath County to take my place."

"You okay leaving your job and coming to work for Jeb?" I said, sensing a little apprehension.

"Depends," J.T. said, leaning back in the booth with his long right arm resting on top of the seat.

"On what?"

"On what Jeb's like to work for," he said.

"We do our jobs then Jeb won't have a problem with anything we do."

"Don't suspect so, since you are his 'fair-haired boy,'" J.T. said.

"That only goes so far," I said. "If I don't do my job he'll fire me, too, just like anyone else that works for him."

"Jeb will never fire you, Cassidy."

"Why is that?"

"Because," J.T. said, smiling, "you're the biggest thing since blue cheese."

"You know, Jeb is my friend, and our boss if you decide to come in on this venture with us. But he's also Sheriff Vogel's friend and has entrusted me…and you…and Dad…to find his son."

"I don't know how much help I can be on this one," J.T. said.

The waitress interrupted us with water and coffee and then took our order. J.T. asked for a B-L-T with hash browns and orange juice and I ordered two eggs sunny side up, ham, toast and orange juice.

"What are you trying to get at?" I said.

"Aw, nothing, Pat, just a little concerned about giving up my job here."

"Is that all?" I said.

"Isn't that enough?"

"Jeb's a good man and he'll take care of us. Besides, you'll be making more money than you could ever earn working around here."

J.T. nodded and went about putting cream and sugar in his coffee.

"J.T.," I said, "I didn't bring down a corrupt politician who was a shoe-in to be elected governor all by myself."

J.T looked up at me and for the first time since I've known him, I caught a glimpse of uncertainty in his eyes. He broke our eye contact and looked out the front window of the café, watching the traffic speed by in both directions.

"Tom Calloway is in jail and Big Jake Riley is dead. Dad and I couldn't have done it without you."

"It's not just that, Pat."

"Then what, for crissakes?"

J.T. was somewhat surprised by the response. He was quiet for a moment as he folded his fingers together, placed his hands on the edge of the table and shrugged his shoulders.

"This thing…looking for Kerry," he said, "is very hard on me."

"Sheriff said the same thing," I said. "Sounds like you both cared for him very much."

"He was my best friend and it's bound to bring up some feelings I shelved away a long time ago."

"Feelings like what?" I said.

"Feelings like…not being able to find him eight years ago…I've let him down."

"How did you let him down?"

J.T. gazed out the front window again, and then reached for his hat.

"I'm leaving, Cassidy, I don't want to talk to you about this right now."

"You can't just leave and walk out on this opportunity," I said.

J.T. put his hat back down in the seat next to him and rubbed his eyes with both hands.

"Damn, Cassidy, you don't know how hard this is for me."

"Yes, I do. Remember…I also lost my best friend."

J.T. straightened and tried to smile as a tall distinguished man with a full head of gray hair walked up to the booth. He was wearing a crisply starched, light blue shirt tucked into khaki trousers.

"J.T.," he said, "good to see you."

"Mayor," J.T. said.

Oh hell, not another mayor.

"Mayor," he said again, "this is my friend, Pat Cassidy. Pat, this is Ted Davenport."

We shook hands.

"Nice to meet you, Pat. I understand you and Jeb Glasscock are stealing J.T. away from us."

"You know how it is…when Jeb makes his mind up it's pretty hard to change it."

"Oh, I know what Jeb Glasscock is like," Davenport laughed. "We've known each other since high school."

"He has his ways," I said, "but Jeb is a good man."

"That he is," Davenport said, "but anyway you look at it, we're losing a fine deputy sheriff."

"Thanks, Mayor," J.T said.

Davenport turned and walked away from our booth and shook hands with the people at the next table. J.T.'s spirit appeared rejuvenated to some degree by the conversation with the Mayor.

"You think I didn't have a lot of doubt in myself trying to figure out why Brett died?" I said.

"I've seen you fight," J.T. said. "I would never believe the man I saw in the ring could ever doubt himself."

"Well, I did. But with Dad's help…and yours…we figured it out…and the men who were responsible have now met their retribution."

"You think we can do it again, Pat?"

"You mean, find Kerry together?"

"Yeah," J.T. said.

"I know we can."

Chapter Three

Late in the afternoon I was back in Fort Worth lacing up the gloves in Panta's Gym preparing to spar with a young, up-and-coming professional heavyweight, by the name of Sammy 'Upper Cut' Johnson. He was a black, twenty-five year old boxer who would earn a ranking among Ring Magazine's elite heavyweights if he won his next fight.

"Watch out for the upper cut," Panta said.

"I've seen him fight," I said.

"If he hits you with it you won't be able to breathe and he'll be all over you."

"I know, Panta."

"He drops his left when he throws the upper cut," Panta said, "and that'll be your opening for that wicked right of yours."

Sammy was waiting for me in the center of the ring when Panta finished tying the strings to the glove on my right hand. 'Upper Cut' was a solid fighter with a well developed upper body on a six-two frame. He donned solid black boxing shorts and shoes. I was wearing my lucky green boxing shorts with a white waist band, white piping and white boxing shoes. Neither of us wore a protective helmet which was becoming more and more popular in boxing circles. In Panta's Gym, wearing a helmet was frowned upon. We tapped gloves and backed away from each other bouncing on the balls of our feet waiting for the sound of the bell to start our three rounds of sparring.

"Take it easy on the amateur," Panta said.

"Yeah, right," Sammy said. "I know better than that."

Sammy pushed his mouthpiece into his mouth and motioned at me with his right hand to 'Come on.'

The first round was spent with me chasing Sammy around the ring and both of us working up a good sweat. The best exchange of punches occurred mid-way through the round when I landed several body shots. He countered with a left hook that found its target solidly against my right temple and followed with a right cross to my left cheek bone. Out of a crouch, I lunged at him with a jolting left jab and then landed a right cross knocking him against the ropes. Sammy bounced back with his own right, but missed badly. He then threw several punches in rapid fire that connected mostly on my shoulders and the outside of my arms that were pulled in to protect my ribs. Once he got out of the corner, I pursued him around the ring dodging his lefts and rights until the round ended.

Sammy grinned widely with a gold tooth showing through the breathing gap in his mouthpiece and gave me a tap on my left shoulder as we retreated to our respective corners.

"Good round," Panta said, encouragingly.

Panta took out the mouthpiece and squirted water across my lips.

"You know he'll try to throw his upper cut this round," he said. "Stay on him…you've got'em on the run. As long as he's backing away from you he won't be able to throw it."

I nodded, took in a deep breath and exhaled as he put the mouthpiece back in.

"Hey, kid," Panta said, as if he were having fun, "this is just like old times."

I nodded my head and moved toward the center of the ring. The bell clanged for round two. Sammy came at me with a barrage of punches. He missed with a double jab, landed a right cross to my right shoulder, snapped a left hook to my jaw, and delivered his patented upper cut. I blocked it with my right arm and grabbed hold of him before he could throw any more punches. We swapped a couple of punches in close.

"Break!" Panta shouted.

Sammy stepped back and threw another right upper cut, but as Panta had pointed out earlier, he always dropped his left when throwing it. I countered with a right cross hitting Sammy square on his chin. He staggered and grabbed me around the outside of my shoulders, holding on tight. I could feel the weakness in his body. Several more body shots drained him even more. Sammy pushed me away and flicked a couple of jabs that bounced off my forehead with little effect. He back peddled using his superior footwork to stay away from me the rest of the round. The bell sounded to end the round. This time Sammy went to his corner without any kind of gesture and without looking at me. His manager, Gino Monzon, climbed through the ropes scolding his fighter.

"What in the hell are you doing out there, Sammy?" he shouted. "Throw your upper cut!"

"Geez, Cassidy," Panta said when I returned to my corner. "You rocked his world with that shot."

The breathing was heavy as he wiped the perspiration from my face with a towel. I mustered up a smile.

"Keep throwing the right, he can't seem to stop it," Panta said.

Round three began with Sammy less enthusiastic to leave the corner than he had been in the first two rounds, as I waited for him at center-ring. His legs appeared to be fine as he danced to my left, staying away from the right hand, but his bottom lip and left eye were swollen. Bobbing and weaving from a crouch, I pinned him against the ropes and landed several shots to his mid-section before he could escape. Sammy moved to his right, sliding against the ropes, when I caught him with another solid right cross. He maneuvered into the corner and covered up, expecting me to hit him again. Instead, I backed away waiting for him to come out of the corner. Sammy advanced forward with both hands in front of him anticipating another right cross. I feigned a right hand then snapped a quick left hook that hit him square on the chin. His knees buckled and his body fell forward grabbing me. Sammy didn't have any fight left in him. The remainder of the round was spent with him trying to land some inside shots. I let him save face by hanging on to him and absorbing the punches.

"You're one helluva a fighter," he said as the round ended.

Sammy left the ring with his head down and Monzon was right behind him giving his fighter the 'what for' as they schlepped toward the locker room.

"Sure you don't want to turn pro?" Panta said as he untied my gloves. "I could get you on the card Monday night in Dallas."

Still breathing hard from the tussle with Sammy, I said, "No, no thanks. I am a little too old to start fighting professionally."

"You're twenty-seven years old," Panta said. "You're not too old…yet."

"Gettin' there though, right?"

"The window of opportunity *is* closing," Panta said.

"Good," I said.

The workout and three rounds with Sammy were exhausting, but my body felt strong and a long shower washed away the fatigue. Clean and groomed, I left Panta's Gym and drove to Dad's house. I refocused on Kerry Vogel as I drove through the traffic of downtown Fort Worth. *In a matter of a month, a kid from a nice family and a stable background goes off to Austin and just disappears?* I had to change lanes and accelerate to get around an orange Vega that slowly puttered out in front of me off Houston Street. I noticed the Texas Rangers bumper sticker on its back bumper. Fourth Street then curved to the left and crossed Fifth Street before it turned into Macon. *Kerry was a real blue-chipper coming out of high school. So, how did he slip through a sieve of media, coaches, and teammates without someone seeing something? Was he seeing someone? Was he hanging out with the wrong people? What happened to you, Kerry Vogel? That's what I have to find out.*

The month of April had arrived without 'The Fool' except for some of the violence around the world. On the radio, WFTW newsman Don Gray reported six bombs exploded in Belfast, Northern Ireland, and twenty new Soviet pilots arrived in Cuba as Castro intervenes militarily in Rhodesia and South Africa. On the other hand, the weather was nice with blue skies, a light westerly wind, and near seventy-five degrees today. *Good day to be at the lake.*

Accelerating onto Interstate 30, Kerry came to mind again. *If his disappearance were a kidnapping, then why would they do it? Sheriff Vogel couldn't possibly afford to pay a ransom that would be worth the price of going to jail. His friend Jeb Glasscock could have.* Veering onto the exit ramp at Camp Bowie Boulevard, I crossed under the overpass and a few blocks later made a right on Dallas Street. *The Sheriff has been living with a lot of pain for a long time. So has J.T. I know exactly how they feel.*

Statuesque live oak and hackberry trees shaded the yards of every home on the block where Dad's house was located. This was the neighborhood where I grew up. The Prewitt boys were playing a game of HORSE in the backyard of their house on the corner. Jackie, Kenneth, and Terry stopped playing basketball long enough to wave enthusiastically. A couple of houses down Mr. Winterowd waved while mowing his grass, and across the street Mrs. Johnson kept an eye on the neighborhood from her front porch. I pulled into the driveway at 1009 N. Dallas Street and parked under the carport.

Home again.

Chapter Four

Emmett Cassidy's home was locked up tight as a drum when I arrived. He was at the lake house enjoying the fishing. Bass and crappie spawn in the spring, and for a serious fisherman like my father, there is no better time of the year. I found the key on my keychain, unlocked the door and went inside. When I turned on the living room lights, the ceiling fan began to spin and the stillness in the room disappeared. My natural inclination was to check to see what there was to eat in the refrigerator. There was always plenty to eat when I lived at home, but that was a long time ago. Since then, Dad has never been one to keep a lot of food around because he eats out so much. Sure enough, the refrigerator was virtually empty except for a six-pack of Miller High Life in the bottle and half a head of iceberg lettuce wrapped in cellophane. *This calls for a trip to Tom's Food Store.*

It was a beautiful late afternoon and the evening held the same promise. The workout and sparring session with Sammy 'Upper Cut' Johnson at Panta's had helped burn away some of the stiffness from being stuck in my car for two and half hours during the drive back from Brownwood, but I still felt like a little more exercise. I decided to walk to the neighborhood grocery store. The sidewalk on our side of the street ran from one end of the block to the other. The Prewitt boys had already gone in for supper. Their basketball sat motionless on the backyard court of dirt and grass. Strolling down the boulevard I passed in front of my mother's best friend's house. Since my mother's passing we hadn't seen much of Peggy Louise Barnes. They had been very close. A lady carrying a small brown paper bag came out of Tom's when I opened the front door. Inside the store, Tom was checking out another customer at the counter, but gave me a nod when he saw me. The shopping carts were lined up along the front wall. I pulled one out and rolled it down the bread aisle and stopped to select a loaf of Mrs. Baird's. At the end of the aisle was a rack of toys that would catch the eye of any six year-old. That included me, as well. I was taught one of my greatest lessons in life right here in this store.

*   *   *

"Where did you get that?" Mom said.

She had walked up behind me on the front porch and caught me playing with my new Zorro knife. It was a small orange pocket knife with the image of Zorro on it. My mother knew how much I had been admiring it on the rack of toys at Tom's. When we would go there, she would shop and I would run down the aisle to see if the Zorro knife was still on display.

"I bought it," I said with a guilty look on my face.

"Pat," Mom said in a firm voice, "where did you get the money to buy the knife?"

"Uh...I don't know."

I think it was about here I knew I was in trouble and began to cry little bitty tears that ran down my cheeks.

"Did you steal it?" Mother said.

I felt awful. I knew I was wrong for stealing the knife and I felt even worse for lying to my mother. I confessed right on the spot to stealing the knife and cried with remorse. My mother drove me to Tom's and had me pay him for the knife and to apologize for my transgression.

"Tom," Mom said, "Pat has something he would like to say to you."

"What's that, Anne?" Tom said, smiling.

"Pat has some money he wants to give you for a knife he took from your toy stand."

"Here's the money, Tom," I said, ashamed to look at him.

"That's not all, Pat," Mom said, "go ahead."

"I'm sorry for stealing the knife," I said through the crying.

"You've done the right thing, Pat," Tom said. "And I hope you've learned your lesson and never do anything like that again."

Mom said the same thing to me on the drive back to the house. I had learned my lesson that day and never again took anything that didn't belong to me.

*   *   *

By the time I worked my way to the meat counter, I had added a jar of Best Maid Pickles, mustard, a large potato, and a head of cabbage to the shopping cart.

Standing behind the meat counter, Tom said, "Been awhile, Pat."

"Yeah, it has," I said.

He reached over the top of the meat display counter and we shook hands. A scale sat at one end of the counter top with a roll of butcher paper next to it. I could only see Tom from the chest upward. His hair had turned mostly gray, but otherwise he looked the same as I remembered. Tom always wore a white apron and today wasn't any different.

"You back in town now?" he said.

"For now," I said. "There's no tellin' what my boss will have me doing in the future."

"How's your dad?"

"He's great. Fishin' at the lake."

"Don't y'all have a place at Palo Pinto?" Tom said.

"Yeah, I can't wait to get back there myself," I said.

"Well, what can I get for you today?"

"I think a pound of homemade klobase will do."

Tom weighed out the sausage links, wrapped them in butcher paper and wrote the price on the outside of the package.

"You ever do anymore boxing?" Tom asked as he checked me out at the cash register.

"Just a little sparring. I still work out at Panta's every chance I get."

"Me and Tom Junior followed your boxing career with a lot of interest."

"Why thanks, Tom. It's always nice to hear that."

He finished entering the prices into the cash register. After each entry, Tom pulled the crank down to enter the price he had punched in. The price would then show up in the register window.

"You being a neighborhood kid and all, we felt like you were part of the family. We'd get the morning paper and check the box scores for the Golden Glove results and there you'd be in the win column every time."

"You're bringing back some old memories now," I said.

"And you know, Pat, I still miss your mother. Anne Cassidy was a great lady."

I watched Tom sack the groceries and thought about my mother. It had been almost fifteen years since her death, but not a day goes by that I don't think of her. This just happened to be the first time today.

"Thanks," I said. "Dad and I still miss her very much."

"She would've been very proud of you, Pat."

Chapter Five

The phone was ringing when I got back to Dad's. I set the sack of groceries down on the kitchen counter and answered the phone hanging on the wall in the den. It was J.T. calling from Brownwood.

"We need to talk about me going to work for you in Fort Worth," he said through the phone line.

"We can do that," I said, sitting down in a swivel rocker. "Let's not rush into anything. You need to make sure this is what you want."

"When you left this morning I was only a little bit unsure, but the more I think about it…the harder this is going to be than I thought."

"Take your time, J.T. I'll probably be in Brownwood come the weekend."

"So what's your next move?" J.T. said.

"I'm going to Austin tomorrow," I said, "to talk to the detective who worked the case back in '68."

"That would be Detective Domingo Perez," J.T. said. "But he's a Texas Ranger now."

The curtains were pulled back from the sliding glass door that led to the backyard. Out beyond the back fence, beyond the back alley, the sun was disappearing behind a thick line of trees.

"You know where you're going to set up an office yet?" J.T. said.

"Why, would that make a difference in your decision?" I said.

"It might," J.T. said.

"In the Glasscock Communication Center down the hall from the radio station," I said.

"What about Brownwood?" J.T. asked.

"That's still a possibility, but I don't want to move to Brownwood any more than you want to move to Fort Worth."

"So…," J.T. said, "which way are you leaning?"

"Fort Worth," I said.

"We'll talk more when you come to Brownwood. Let me know what you find out in Austin."

The conversation with J.T. was over and it was suppertime. I went back into the kitchen and took the groceries out of the large paper sack. *First things first, though.* Opening the refrigerator, I took out a Miller High Life and popped the cap with the bottle opener mounted on the inside of the pantry door. The cold beer tasted really good. I took out a cutting board from behind the bread box and a butcher knife from the utility drawer and placed them on the kitchen counter. With beer in hand, I went into the living room and turned on the television to Channel 8. Murphy Martin was anchoring the news of the day. My eyes were fixed on the TV screen but my mind was on Paula Conn, a reporter for Channel 8 that I had gotten to know. She was now in New York working for a major network. Then, I thought about Kerry Vogel again. *Are you dead or alive? Your dad and J.T. couldn't find you…the*

Austin P.D. couldn't find you. Where...are...you? You've vanished off the face of the earth. Why? There is no evidence of foul play...except...you're missing.

My father has a pragmatic philosophy about life and he always says that a man's fall from grace is pretty simple. It's always one of two things...either 'Punch or Judy.' The 'Punch' being too much drink; the 'Judy' being too much woman. Kerry's disappearance would probably fall into one of those categories as well.

I picked up the TV Guide to see what was on the tube tonight. *There are just too many choices these days.* At seven o'clock I could watch *Welcome Back, Kotter,* or *The Waltons. Hmmm...I like John Boy and the family better than Kotter...but I want to watch Barney Miller at seven thirty.* It would be an easier decision to make at eight o'clock. *Hawaii Five-O* hands down. I had a tough choice at nine o'clock though. Would it be *The Streets of San Francisco* or *Barnaby Jones?*

A little while later I was sitting in Dad's recliner watching *Barney Miller* and enjoying another beer with my supper in front of me on a TV tray. *Since I don't think Kerry vanished because of 'Punch,' I'll bet anything it had something to do with 'Judy.'*

Book 'em, Dano.

Chapter Six

A little before noon the traffic on Interstate 35 near the University of Texas was almost at a standstill. Texas Ranger Domingo Perez said he would meet me for lunch at an out of the way restaurant in East Austin called Sam's Bar-B-Cue. Ranger Perez said it was easy to find. Take the 12th Street exit off the interstate, turn left, and Sam's was ten blocks further. The parking lot was full, but I found a place to park a half a block away on Poquito Street, which in Spanish means little. Poquito was true to its translation. Sam's was located in an old white building with a high tin roof, a brown brick smokestack, and green trim. The Pepsi sign hanging out front said, "Sam's BBQ…Serving Austin's Original Meat Sausage." As I rounded the corner, Ranger Perez walked up from the other direction carrying a briefcase and dressed in a stiffly starched long sleeve green shirt and dark green slacks. Perez donned a straw cowboy hat and had a Colt .45 semiautomatic on his right hip. His round silver badge with a star was pinned to his left pocket and identified him as a Texas Ranger by words and its unique shape.

"Cassidy?" he said.

"Yes, sir," I said. "How did you know it was me?"

"Easy," Perez said. "I'm a Texas Ranger. I'm a trained eagle-eye." He laughed at his joke. "Saw you when you turned the corner.

You were easy to spot. After all, you've been on the news a lot these days."

I stuck out my right hand and we shook.

"Did you bring Kerry's file?" I said.

"Sure thing," Perez said. "Austin P.D. was more than happy to oblige after I told them who it was for. We're all just glad you brought down that Calloway son-of-a-bitch. Can you imagine what he would have been like as our governor?"

"No, I can't," I said.

"Brought along my own personal file from the case, too," Perez said. "Let's go on in…Sam's holdin' a booth for us."

"That's awfully nice of him considering the place looks to be packed."

"It is…always is at lunch. But hell, kid, I'm a Texas Ranger," Perez said, laughing at his own joke again.

The smell of barbecue and all the fixins' inundated the dining room. Perez and I sat on opposite sides of the booth where a waitress brought us six slices of white bread, a plate of pickles and onions, barbecue sauce, and asked what we would like to drink. We both ordered sweet tea.

"Normally you have to order your food over there," Perez said, pointing at the 'Place Order Here" sign, "but Sam knows Pat Cassidy is eating lunch at his place today."

"Geez…I feel honored," I said.

"Should be…Sam doesn't get all goo-goo for celebrities very often. The last one he bent over backwards for was Joplin."

"Scott or Janis?" I said.

"Janis," Perez cracked. "Sam ain't that damn old."

"What's that about fifteen minutes of fame?" I said.

"It's more than fame," Perez said, "it's how you did it and what you did. If you're ever interested in Rangerin'…let me know. You'd make a good one."

"You'll be the first to know," I said.

Perez opened up his briefcase and took out two manila folders and laid them in the middle of the red and white checkered tablecloth. A black waitress wearing a red t-shirt under denim blue overalls with a bandana tied around her neck brought us tea and took our order. Perez asked for a sausage sandwich and I ordered sliced brisket. Both came with beans and potato salad.

"How is Sheriff Vogel these days?" Perez said.

"He wants to find his son."

"Well at least that hasn't changed. He called me once a month, like clockwork, until I left the department for the Rangers."

"Then he quit calling?"

"No, then he started calling my former partner."

"What do *you* think happened to him?"

"Cassidy, I have no earthly idea what happened to this boy."

"You have any *un*earthly idea what might have happened to him?" I said.

Perez started to say something; then he stopped and smiled. "Unearthly?" he said. "I suppose you mean…do I have a gut feeling?"

"Yeah, gotta hunch?" I said.

"I think the boy stumbled onto something and got whacked. Was where he wasn't supposed to be…witnessed something…was at the wrong place at the wrong time. You know what I mean, don't you?"

"I know exactly what you mean," I said, thinking of my best friend, Brett. "Tell me what you do know."

"That would be very little, but here's what I've got. Kerry lived at the freshman football player's dorm. He ate breakfast at 6:30 a.m. in the cafeteria, went to morning practice at eight, had lunch at the cafeteria, went to afternoon practice at four, and was in the cafeteria for supper at seven. He never missed a meal and never missed a practice."

"Sheriff Vogel says Kerry was late for practice a few times," I said.

"Roommate says he was on the pay phone down the hall from their dorm room when he left for practice more than once. Roomy said he was late getting to practice each time and it caused him to have to run extra wind sprints."

"What's the roommate's name?"

"Jerry Don Lane…he's an investment banker in San Antonio now."

"Did he say who Kerry was talking to?"

"No," Perez said, "but he did say he heard the name Charlie."

"That's all you got?"

"I'm afraid so."

"Sheriff Vogel also said Kerry was acting like something was on his mind other than football," I said.

"That's what Coach Earl told me. What he actually said was Kerry's heart didn't seem to be in the game."

"Did Lane mention anything about how he was acting?"

"Only that he was being secretive about the phone calls and always lowered his voice when someone walked by him."

"Then…the name Charlie is all we've got," I said.

"Ain't that a bitch," Perez said.

"What do you mean?"

"What I mean is a Texas Ranger, the Austin P.D., the Brown County Sheriff and the law enforcement network in the whole damn United States can't come up with one iota of stinkin' evidence to find that boy. Here it is eight years later and we still can't tell you whether Charlie is a man or a woman."

"It's probably a woman."

"What makes you think that?"

"A hunch," I said.

"Yeah, well, a lot a good that'll do ya. A hunch and six-bits will get you into the new Texas Ranger Museum in Waco."

Out of Touch

The waitress brought our food. Perez picked up the folders and set them off to the side of the table and took a bite of his sausage sandwich. I cut into the brisket, ate a bite and then tasted the potato salad. *Excellent!*

Chapter Seven

In the middle of the afternoon I sat in the University of Texas coach's office waiting to talk to Mike Earl, Kerry Vogel's recruiter. The walls of the office were burnt orange and decorated with black and white pictures of Longhorn All-Americans and national championship teams. The secretary told me Earl was in a meeting with the head coach and would meet with me as soon as he could. I smiled at her which appeared to please her. She then smiled back which I also found very pleasing. The name plate on her desk said she was Linda Preston. Linda was an attractive woman, about my age, with long blonde hair parted down the middle. Her slim figure was dressed in a powder blue sleeveless blouse tucked into a cream colored short skirt. Her arms and legs were lean and tanned.

"Just curious, Mr. Cassidy," she said, with her green eyes peering at me, "why are you here to see Coach Earl?"

"Pat," I said.

"Excuse me?" she said.

"Call me Pat."

"Oh, O.K. My name's Linda."

"Kerry Vogel," I said. "Do you remember him?"

"Yes, he was supposed to be the next great Texas quarterback. He was in my ex-husband's recruiting class."

"Was your ex-husband a coach or player?"

"Player," Linda said. "He was a running back."

"What's his name?" I said.

"Billy Preston."

"You were married to Billy Preston?" I said.

"Yes."

"All-American running back drafted by the Giants?"

"The same," Linda said, looking at a picture on her desk.

"He got hurt last year," I said. "How is the rehab coming along?"

"It's made him even meaner than he was." She picked up a picture of a little boy and showed it to me. "This is our son, Billy Junior."

I looked at the picture of Billy Junior who appeared to be about eight years old.

"Cute kid," I said.

"It was a rotten marriage, but we have a great son."

Two men came out of an office behind Linda's desk. I recognized Darrell King, the head coach, who turned around and went back into his office. Mike Earl stopped at Linda's desk.

"Coach Earl," Linda said, "Pat Cassidy is here to see you."

"Cassidy," he said, shaking my hand, "come on in my office."

Mike Earl turned and walked toward his office and I followed him.

I looked back at Linda and said, "Good luck with that kid. He looks like a real winner."

"Thanks," she said, smiling. "I think I'll keep him."

Mike Earl sat at his desk and invited me to sit down.

"So, Mr. Cassidy, you wanna talk about Kerry Vogel."

His voice carried a Midwest accent and the resonance of it rolled around in my head.

"Illinois," I said.

"Illinois?" Earl said. "Oh, yeah, the accent. But I'm from Indiana. Valparaiso to be exact."

"Tell me about Kerry Vogel," I said.

"What would you like to know about him?"

"What made you want to recruit him?"

"Kerry Vogel was the best QB in the state the year we recruited him. Best numbers of any quarterback we looked at *and* he led his high school team to a state championship."

"His dad told me you became very close," I said.

"We were, but I always get close to the kids I wanna sign."

Earl's dark brown shirt with white stitching, brown slacks, white shoes, and white belt were attempting to make a fashion statement, but missed the point. His complexion was weathered and his blonde hair was ruffled and windblown. Earl leaned back in his chair with his hands laced together behind his head.

"He was a great kid and a great talent," Earl said. "Wish they could all be like him. I'm sorry things happened the way they did…he would have been a great asset to our program."

"You mean the way he disappeared?" I asked.

"Yes, of course."

"Coach, you were closer to Kerry than anyone here. What was going on with him?"

"The best I can recall is he didn't seem to have it the moment he stepped onto the practice field."

"Kerry had lost heart," I said. "Isn't that odd?"

"Not really," Earl said. "Some kids can't make the transition from high school to college ball."

"Isn't that something you look for when you recruit a kid?"

"Yes, but it's not a perfect science."

"Did you see any inkling that it would happen with Kerry?"

"Absolutely not," Earl said. "I believed he was as solid a recruit as we've ever had."

"Did it ever enter your mind something might be wrong?"

Earl's relaxed, kicked back position shifted to one of crossed arms as he rocked slightly in his chair.

"Cassidy, once we get these kids on campus there has to be some natural attrition. If they don't want to give it 'their all' then we've got to weed them out. It takes a lot of heart in a player to win a national championship."

"That's what it's all about, isn't it?" I said.

"You mean the winning?" Earl said.

"Yes, I mean the winning."

"I follow boxing and I know firsthand what you did in the ring," Earl said. "You telling me you didn't have a champion's heart? Did those titles you won not mean anything to you?"

"Touché," I said. "Sheriff Vogel said when he left for Austin he was the same kid."

"That may be the case," Earl said, "but Kerry had changed by the time we got him."

"How much time elapsed from when he checked into the dorm and two-a-days began?" I said.

"Freshman orientation for incoming athletes takes a week," Earl said.

"Kerry leaves Brownwood on Saturday morning…"

"He signed in at eleven-thirty a.m. according to our records," Earl said, finishing my sentence.

"And he has the rest of the weekend on his own," I said.

"Most of the boys come with their families."

"But Kerry wasn't most boys."

"No, he wasn't," Earl said. "He had an independent streak."

"What about freshman orientation week? Anything scheduled in the evenings to occupy their time?"

"Full week of activities," Earl said.

"Did Kerry attend any of them?"

"Don't know…the boys weren't required to sign in for that kind of stuff."

"Who would know?"

"Maybe his roommate."

"Jerry Don Lane," I said.

"Sounds like you've done your homework," Earl said, a little surprised I knew about him.

"Some," I said, "but a good reporter once told me, that when you don't have answers…ask questions."

"Sage advice," Earl said.

"It was."

Chapter Eight

The Holiday Inn was located a few blocks from downtown Austin on the Colorado River and just off I-35. My room was on the fourth floor overlooking the river. Dim lights on each side of the dresser mirror illuminated the room just enough for me to see where to put everything. I placed the suitcase on the bed, hung the hanging clothes in the closet, and put the briefcase on the table in the corner. The air conditioner hummed faintly in front of the window and the curtains blocked the light of the day. The late afternoon sunlight immediately brightened the room when I pulled back the curtains. There would be a beautiful sunset in a few hours if I were going to be here to see it. But I had plans to do more research at the UT Library. I took off my blue blazer and hung it up in the closet. The shoulder strap and holstered nine millimeter was next. I slipped out of it and put it on the shelf in the closet. I changed out of a white dress shirt and khakis into a black t-shirt, jeans, and blue jean jacket and headed back to the UT campus.

The traffic bottlenecked near the downtown exits and slowed to a snail's pace. *Kerry Vogel was having secretive phone calls with someone named Charlie. Was Charlie a man or woman?* Texas Ranger Domingo Perez told me he thought Kerry was probably in the wrong place at the wrong time, and because of that, may have been murdered.

Conjecture on his part. According to the Austin P.D. file on the case, the investigation into Kerry's disappearance had been thorough enough. All students with the first names Charles, Charlie, Chuck, Chad or Charlene had been interviewed and dismissed as possible suspects. Perez's personal file on the case showed he left no stone unturned. *So, who in the hell is Charlie?* My visit with Mike Earl had revealed almost nothing of use…except that Kerry's roommate, Jerry Don Lane, might be able to shed a little light on what he was up to during freshman orientation week. In a short period of time Kerry went from being a highly recruited high school quarterback with unlimited potential, to a kid who Coach Earl described as…not having the heart to play the game anymore. *Why?* As the northbound lane of I-35 crept along, I turned on the radio and dialed up a local country station.

"Austin's *Home for Country Music*…you're listening to 1490 K-B-E-T and here's Johnny Duncan with 'Charlie is My Name.'"

The words to the song drove home an overpowering feeling that Charlie wasn't just any Charlie. *Sorry Charlie.* But Charlie has to be a girl. What else would cause a football player to lose his hard-nosed edge? *Other than drugs or Jesus.* Kerry may have gotten messed up in drugs all right; however, a little pot smoking doesn't necessarily mean a drug problem. The religion thing isn't even on the radar, but it's been known to happen. I recall an All-American and All-Pro football player who once told me he found Jesus ten years after he quit playing ball. He said Jesus taught him to lift up his opponents instead of knocking them down. Maybe Kerry learned that lesson sooner than he did. There is a possibility that we could be dealing with all three, but I kind of doubt it. The odds of Kerry falling in love, getting religion, and becoming a victim of drug abuse seemed, for the moment, farfetched.

The UT Library was busy with students coming and going with books in hand. Study groups clustered together, some with their noses buried in books, others quietly discussing and debating the latest teachings of academia. A student who worked for the library helped me locate microfilm of the Austin American Statesman from June, July, and August of 1968.

In the corner of the microfilm room I began to search through the film. The front pages of June, 1968, were dominated by news of Robert F. Kennedy's assassination. Helen Keller, who overcame blindness and deafness, died at age 87, and Andy Warhol was shot and wounded by radical feminist, Valarie Solanas.

On June eighth a headline read "James Earl Ray Arrested for Murder of Martin Luther King." It made me think of Dion DiMucci's song 'Abraham, Martin, and John'.

Has anybody here…seen my old friend Martin…Can you tell me where he's gone? He freed a lot of people, but it seems the good, they die young…But I just looked around and he's gone…

On the sports pages, Denny McClain beat the Red Sox on June fifth to improve to nine and one and Dock Ellis pitched a no-hitter for the Pittsburgh Pirates on June twelfth. McClain would win thirty games in 1968; Ellis would win six. After a couple of hours I had worked my way to the August eighth edition of the Statesman, when I noticed a small advertisement in the bottom right hand corner of the classified section.

It read, "Come hear Sister Charlene from the Church of the Chosen and become the kind of person you never dreamed you could be. Revival August 8-14."

I stared at the ad for a long time. *Charlene. Could this be Charlie?* Opening up my notebook on Kerry's case, I looked at the timeline of events leading up to his disappearance. The day he moved to Austin was August eighth. After studying the advertisement a little longer, I went to find the helpful student to show me how to make a copy of the page off the microfilm.

As I left the library through the front door and walked down the steps, I looked up and saw Kelly Glasscock walking toward me.

Uh-oh.

Chapter Nine

Kelly Glasscock sat across the table from me in the Front Room of Scholz Garten on San Jacinto Street in downtown Austin. She leaned forward and, with the slender fingers of her left hand, made a swishing motion that brushed my hair to the side and away from my forehead.

"There…that's better," Kelly said. "I think this is the longest I've ever seen your hair."

"It is," I said.

"Is this the new you?"

"No…just need a trim. That's all."

Kelly's long blonde hair was in a braid to the middle of her back and her hazel eyes were captivating. A few freckles spotted the smooth skin around her cheekbones and her makeup was freshly applied and on target. As always, her smile was flirty but always authentic. Kelly's natural beauty was breathtaking and something was pulling us together. I was not sure what it was, but the chemistry we seemed to have going on between us was mercurial.

"Dad said you were in town," Kelly said, "and for you to call him…in case I was to *bump* into you."

"Did you know I was going to be at the library?" I said.

"Pat, I know in the past there have been times when I knew where you were going to be, but this time it was a coincidence."

Kelly was wearing a white UT baseball undershirt with burnt orange sleeves tucked into her tight blue jeans. The sleeves of the jersey stopped halfway between her elbows and wrists and she had on a pair of white tennis shoes.

"I'm glad I bumped into you," I said.

"Me, too," Kelly said.

The waitress arrived at our table with a basket of freshly baked rolls and took our drink orders. I ordered a Shiner Bock on tap and a white wine spritzer for Kelly.

"What did you find out at the library about your case?" Kelly asked.

"Not much," I said. "Read a lot about what happened in June, July, and August of 1968."

"Gosh," Kelly said, "I was fourteen years old then."

"I was nineteen."

"You see," she said, "there's not that much difference in our ages."

"I've known that all along, but back then you would've been jail bait."

"That was a long time ago, Pat."

Kelly picked up a roll and tore it in half, took a small bite, and put the rest of it on a white paper napkin.

"You look like your mother with your hair back in a braid," I said.

"Just what every girl wants to hear," Kelly said, "that she looks like her mother."

"You have a beautiful mother, Kelly, and of the three Glasscock daughters, you look the most like her."

"Not to change the subject, but have you thought any more about us dating after I graduate?"

"I have," I said.

"Mom and Dad don't have a problem with us seeing each other."

"That doesn't take away from the fact you are Jeb's daughter and that is a huge hurdle for me to get over," I said.

The waitress reappeared and put the spritzer with a slice of lime in front of Kelly and then placed a dark beer near my right hand. I took a drink of the Shiner.

"There is an attraction," I said. "I can't deny that, but you are like…the forbidden fruit."

"The fruit is ripe for the picking," Kelly said.

"So you mean I can take a bite of the apple."

Kelly smiled and said, "Anytime you're ready."

"How is that boyfriend of yours?"

"I broke up with him," Kelly said. "Larry is in the past now."

"How long have you been apart?"

"Since that day I left you at the ranch."

"Last month," I said.

"Yes," Kelly said. "I knew if I was ever going to have a chance with you I had to end it."

"How'd he take it?"

"Not well and to make matters worse," Kelly paused and looked around the room, "I get the feeling he's following me."

I know the feeling.

Scholz Garten was quiet for a Tuesday evening. We were at a table near the bar, which made it easy to watch *Police Woman* on the television set elevated behind the bar. *Angie Dickinson has always been easy to watch!* The light yellow walls were decorated with antique signs mostly of German heritage, with a few lighted beer signs and framed Texas Longhorn team spirit posters interspaced among them. The floors were natural hardwood and a wide doorway behind me led to the historic Biergarten. A picture of the 1893 University of Texas football team, the first in school history to go unbeaten, hung on the wall near the end of the bar next to a picture of August Scholz, the founder of Scholz Garten.

"Has he threatened you?" I said.

"No, but I have seen him in places I know he shouldn't be," Kelly said. "Different places around campus. After all, I know his schedule, and when he's somewhere at a certain time when he's supposed to be on the other side of the campus, then he's not where he's supposed to be. You know what I mean?"

"Umm...I think so," I said.

"It's not something I can't handle, Pat. Anyway, Larry's a pussycat. He's not a tough guy like you."

Returning with a pad in one hand and a blue Bic pen in the other, the waitress asked if we were ready to order. Kelly, nor I, had even looked at the menu.

"Give us a few more minutes," I said, flashing a smile.

The somewhat attractive young woman smiled back and said, "Sure, take your time," and walked away.

Kelly reached out and touched my hands with the tips of her fingers. The room became a little warmer and I had an almost uncontrollable urge to kiss her. Her complexion took on an amorous glow, especially in the area of her cheekbones and freckles. Maybe it was because of the wine, maybe it was because of me, or maybe it was because of both the wine and me. Either way it was a beautiful sight.

"Do you know what happened to my last girlfriend?" I said.

"Of course I do, Pat. I read the papers and watch TV."

"I wouldn't want something like that to happen to you," I said.

Kelly smiled brightly with amusement in her eyes.

"Pat, I know you would never hurt me."

"Not intentionally," I said. "But with some of the things that go on around me innocent people quite often get hurt."

"I'm not afraid," Kelly said.

"That's easy to say," I said, "but I could never forgive myself if anything was to happen to you because of me."

"Like I said, Pat…"

"Yeah, yeah, yeah," I said, "you're not afraid. The fact remains, I'm not looking for a steady relationship in my life right now."

Kelly leaned forward, and in a little louder than a whisper said, "It won't always be that way."

"But for now, Kelly, I have issues."

"Because of what happened to Brett Tucker," Kelly said.

"Yes," I said, drumming my fingers on the table top.

She put her hands over mine as if the drumming annoyed her and forced a smile.

"And," I said, shrugging, "everything else that happened."

The somewhat attractive waitress walked by with a tray of drinks in her hands and I waved her over to let her know we were ready to order. Kelly chose a Chef Salad from the menu and I selected a Corned Beef and Swiss on Rye. It came with chips and I ate the sandwich and all the chips, washing them down with another Shiner Bock. Kelly ate very little of her salad.

After we finished our meal we left the restaurant and walked south on San Jacinto Avenue where our cars were parked a half a block away. A man got out of a 1974 Gran Torino and walked slowly toward us. Sensing trouble, I stopped and turned to face Kelly. Firmly holding her shoulders, I looked her in the eyes and said, "Be ready for anything. If I say run…go back inside and call the police."

Kelly looked at me and then at the shadowy figure walking toward us.

"Don't get all worked up, Pat. It's only Larry."

"What is he doing here?" I said.

"What do you think?"

She stepped a couple of feet in front of me and shouted at him as he walked in our direction. "Larry, you're going to have to quit following me!"

Larry stopped and said with a nervous voice, "Is this the guy you broke up with me for?"

"No, Larry," Kelly said, "he's just a friend."

He moved toward us circling to our right with his back to the street. Larry put his hands on his hips and dropped his head.

"It's Pat Cassidy, isn't it?" he said.

Larry was a good inch shorter than Kelly even in his boots, which put him at about five feet eight inches tall. He had long black hair to his shoulders and wore a tight green t-shirt that displayed muscular arms.

"I knew it, Kelly," Larry said. "I knew it from the moment you broke up with me. It was always about Pat Cassidy, your high school crush that's the *big* hero."

"That's enough, Larry," Kelly said. "You need to leave or I'm going to call the police."

"You don't need to do that, Kelly," I said. "I can take care of him right here and now."

"Come on, you son-of-a-bitch," Larry said, taunting me.

Larry doubled up his fists as I moved around Kelly to get to him. She put her body between Larry and me when he launched a looping right hand. I pushed Kelly out of the way, but before I could avoid the punch, it landed, glancing off my left eye. The expression on Larry's face was one of horror. I can only imagine what must have been going through his mind. He had just punched a former National Golden Gloves champion in the eye. Larry might have also been thinking that this is the guy who shot and killed his last girlfriend. While he was surprised the punch actually landed, I was just as surprised that a pussycat, as Kelly called him, was able to hit me without me putting up any kind of defense. He stood frozen and as I stared at him, I wasn't really sure what to do. If I threw a punch I would probably knock him out. So instead, I shoved him in the chest with the palms of my hands as hard as I could.

"Pat, no!" Kelly shouted.

Larry flew back across the hood of the car parallel parked behind him and slid off into the street. Kelly ran to Larry and helped him to his feet.

"How could you do this, Pat?" Kelly said. "I told you I could handle this. Now you've hurt him."

I just looked at Kelly in disbelief. Larry put his arm over Kelly's shoulders and leaned against her as they staggered their way to his car. As she opened the passenger side door of the Gran Torino, Larry looked back at me and I thought I saw a glimpse of a smile before he flopped down onto the front seat. Kelly got in on the driver's side without looking at me, or saying a word, and drove off with him.

Is this for real?

Chapter Ten

The man behind the front desk said there were a couple of messages for me when I got back to the Holiday Inn on the River. One of the messages was from Kelly.

It said, "Call me."

The other message was from Jeb.

It said, "First chance you get, call me."

I was sure one had nothing to do with the other. In my room I put my notes from the library on the night stand next to the phone and slipped out of my tennis shoes. I fluffed up one of the pillows on the bed and propped it up on top of the other pillow. Leaning back, I picked up the phone and called Domingo Perez at his residence. After a couple rings he answered.

"I have a couple of questions for you," I said.

"Shoot...not literally, though," he joked.

"Ever heard of a religious group called the Church of the Chosen?"

"Sounds familiar," Perez said. "Why?"

"I found an advertisement about them in an August '68 edition of the Statesman. They held a revival the week Kerry Vogel disappeared. The ad said come to hear Sister Charlene and discover the kind of person you never thought you could be."

"You think she's our Charlie?"

"I don't know…what do you think?"

"I think anything is possible but I'd be surprised we'd miss something that obvious. Where was the ad?"

"The classified section," I said. "A small advertisement located in the bottom right hand corner of the page."

"Geez, Cassidy, don't you have a social life?"

"Of course I do."

"Then why in the hell are you digging through microfilm when you could be meeting good-looking coeds running around all over this town?"

"I did both," I said. "Had time to do my work and have dinner with a beautiful Texas cheerleader."

"Oh," Perez said.

He was quiet for a moment.

"Damn, boy, you work fast," Perez chuckled. "O.K., where were we?"

"The advertisement in the Austin American-Statesman," I said.

"Cassidy, that was my case back then and my partner and I skimmed the paper every day hoping to find something that would shed a little light on Kerry's disappearance."

"You almost would have to be looking for it to see it," I said.

"How did *you* know to look for it if you didn't know it was there?" Perez asked.

"The more I scanned through the microfilm the more I felt like I was near something."

"I've heard that about you," Perez said.

"Heard what?"

"That you have an uncanny knack to sense things."

"It's a gift," I said.

"Sounds like a curse to me," Perez said. "Either way, it'll come in handy if you plan on finding Kerry."

"So, Ranger Perez, think this could be our Charlie?"

"Cassidy, to tell you the truth we may have missed a few things in Kerry's disappearance. We were overworked like crazy during the summer of '68. Most of us were working special detail at the LBJ Ranch as well as our fulltime jobs at the Austin PD and didn't know which end was coming or going. After the RFK assassination, the Secret Service called in as much extra help as they possibly could to protect the President's ranch."

"I understand, Ranger, the President's security was a lot more important than one missing young man from Brownwood, Texas."

"It wasn't that we forgot about Kerry," Perez said.

He was silent for a moment and I could hear a woman's voice in the background.

"But," Perez continued, "we may have overlooked a few things."

"So, what's your hunch about this Sister Charlene?" I said.

"I think what you've come up with is a great piece of detective work. Follow your lead."

Perez hung up. It was too late to call Jeb, so I put that off until first thing in the morning. As far as Kelly's message was concerned, that would have to wait, indefinitely.

Chapter Eleven

After breakfast in the hotel restaurant, I went back upstairs to my room and called Jeb. It was a quarter till seven as I sat on the edge of the bed and dialed his number at the ranch in Brownwood. Maria, his housekeeper, answered the phone and went to get him.

"How's Austin?" Jeb said when he picked up the receiver.

"Making headway on Kerry's disappearance, I think."

"Good," Jeb said. "Can you come to the ranch soon?"

"Why, what's up?"

"Gotta couple of things to discuss with ya," Jeb said. "I want ya to look at a place here and see if you'd be interested in settin' up your headquarters in Brownwood instead of Fort Worth."

"I don't know if I want to do that, Jeb."

"Look at it this way, Pat. You're workin' for me and this way you'll be dealin' directly with me. That way when we discuss things we'll be doin' it in person…and not over the phone. There'll be less of a misunderstandin' if you can look me in the eyes and read my face."

"I'll come to Brownwood and discuss it with you but I'm pretty dead-set on setting up our office at the Glasscock Communications Center in Fort Worth."

"All I want ya to do is hear me out," Jeb said.

"I can probably be there this weekend," I said.

"Great," Jeb said. "See ya Saturday."

Kerry's file was in my briefcase on the desk near the window. I pulled out the file and took out his 1968 High School Graduation picture and the printout from the library. Kerry was a handsome kid. His vital statistics were brown hair, brown eyes, six feet-one inch tall and, at the time of his disappearance, he weighed one hundred and eighty-seven pounds. The black and white photograph was taken with Kerry wearing a dark jacket with a white shirt and dark bow-tie. When I looked through Kerry's senior yearbook, I noticed every male in the graduating class was wearing the same outfit. His facial features were strong with a lot of hair combed nicely, high cheek bones, high forehead, and prominent chin. Kerry's eyes were closely set and appeared to be searching for fun. I put the picture down and picked up the library printout. The advertisement on the bottom right side of the page gave the address for the church at a location in East Austin. I wrote it down and placed the printout and picture back in the folder and closed the briefcase.

The building that was once the Church of the Chosen stood on a street corner four blocks past Albert Sidney Johnston High School. The small white frame structure was boarded up with a sign on the front door that said 'no trespassing.' Weeds inundated the yard area on both sides of a wide walkway leading to the front steps. Thick ivy overpowered un-kept bushes and climbed up the facade of the abandoned church toward a tattered roof. I parked along the curb and thought about what I should do next. Glancing up the block, I noticed a hand painted sign extending out from the front of a house with a white roof and blue aluminum siding. It read, "Buddy's Grocery Store." Buddy's appeared to be operated from a long rectangular room that had been added on to the front of the house to accommodate the small neighborhood convenience store. I got out of the Malibu and walked down the street to the front door of Buddy's Grocery Store. The screening on the dirty white door had been patched in several places and a cowbell announced my presence as I opened it. In the far corner of the room a man sat behind a small wooden desk.

"Come in," he said, smiling.

His gray hair was cut in a flat-top and his gray eyes roamed the room aimlessly as he looked in my direction. The man was blind. He leaned a little to his left and momentarily searched for the knob on an old radio to turn the volume down. I walked the short distance from the door, with the cowbell clanging behind me, and stood in front of him.

"What can I do for you young man?" he said with his sightless eyes peering at me as if he could see me.

"Interesting," I said. "You're blind, but yet you knew I was not only a man, but a young man."

"Easy, son," he said, "your boots make the sound of a full grown man and your cologne tells me your age."

"So, how old am I?"

"You're probably twenty-four, maybe twenty-five and your cologne is British Sterling."

"Close enough. My name is Pat Cassidy."

He held out his hand, I took hold of it firmly, and shook.

"My name's Buddy Connor. You wouldn't by any chance be the Mr. Cassidy that was involved with that political scandal last month, would you?"

"One and the same," I said. "Please, call me Pat."

"Well…whoooo doggies…sit down," Buddy said, "and have a Coke on me."

"Thanks, but instead of a Coke, how about some information?"

"Sure," Buddy said, still holding the smile he greeted me with when I first came into the store.

Buddy was to my right as I sat down in a squeaky straw-back chair in front of his makeshift counter. My left elbow rubbed against an ice cream chest as I sat down. A Frigidaire on the other side of the front window had a sign taped to the door listing its contents; milk, butter, and cheese. Another sign on the wall behind Buddy listed the soft drinks available in the Coca-Cola ice chest. Coke, Dr. Pepper, Triple X Root Beer, Seven Up, and Nehi Orange and Grape Drinks were all twenty-five cents each. A living room area was visible through the door behind the ice chest. Shelves with an assortment of canned goods and household products filled the wall on the other side of the doorway. A lonely cigarette machine at the opposite end of the room was mirrored at the top allowing me to see the upper part of my head. *It appears a haircut will be in order soon.*

"What's on your mind?" Buddy said.

"The old church down the street," I said, "didn't it used to be the Church of the Chosen?"

"Sure did…six, seven years back. It might have even been a little longer ago than that."

"What happened to it?" I asked. "Did they move to another location?"

Buddy wobbled his head in a motion the way people with no sight often do, and said, "Oh, it closed up right after their one and only revival. They weren't there very long and after that it was one church after another, until about two years ago when the owner boarded it up."

"Who owns the building?" I said.

"The man who owned it back then," Buddy said, "is dead. Don't have any idea who owns it now. Last I heard, the city had condemned the place and was going to tear it down."

"Remember anything about Sister Charlene?"

"Oh, yeah," Buddy said with a curious grin, "back then the guys told me she was a real looker."

He leaned forward and put his elbows on his desk, clasped his hands together, and pointed his eyes toward mine. He smiled widely.

"One day she came in and tried to recruit me for her revival. Said she could heal me if I believed strong enough. I laughed at her. I told her she might have a better chance healing the cow that kicked me in the head more than she would me."

"I take it you didn't go to the revival," I said.

"No," Buddy said, "but, there was something about her voice that was a real turn on. Hell…I had a hard on by the time she left."

"What did they say she looked like?"

"She had a beautiful face they tell me. Face like an angel. Guys around here described her as having long beautiful blonde hair, blue eyes, and the body of a goddess."

"Were there any converts from the neighborhood?" I said.

"A few of the guys went just to see what was going on, but mostly just to look at her. No conversions that I remember."

"After the revival and the Church of the Chosen closed down, what happened to Sister Charlene?"

"Don't know for sure, man, but I heard her church was from Houston. I always figured she went back there."

"Thanks, Buddy, you've been a great help," I said.

"Why all the questions, Pat?"

"I'm looking for someone who disappeared back around the same time the 'Chosen' was holding their revival."

"Must be someone really important," Buddy said.

"He is," I said.

Out of Touch

"Hey, you got a minute?" Buddy said. "I wanna show you a little trick I've learned since that cow kicked me in the eyes and cataracts took my sight."

"Sure, Buddy, I'm not in any kind of hurry."

"You got any cash on you?"

"Yeah," I said.

"Give me two or three different denominations, if you've got'em."

Removing the wallet from my back left pocket, I opened it up and pulled out a five, twenty, and hundred dollar bill and handed them to Buddy.

"Now...," he said, feeling of the five dollar bill with the finger tips of both hands, "...this one is an old Abe Lincoln."

He handed the five dollar bill back to me and picked up the twenty.

"This one is a twenty," Buddy said, placing it down on the counter top and sliding it toward me.

I picked up the twenty and with the five put them back in my wallet.

"And this one is...," Buddy rubbed his fingers over the hundred dollar bill and grinned like a possum, "...an old Ben Franklin. Don't get many of these in this neighborhood."

Buddy tried to hand the hundred dollar bill back to me.

"Keep it," I said.

"What?" Buddy said, surprised.

"The show was worth it," I said. "Thanks for the information and if you remember anything else you can reach me at the Holiday Inn on the River."

"Thank you, Pat. I will…I'll ask around and if anyone tells me something that would be useful to you I'll call you."

"Nice to meet you, Buddy."

"Likewise, and it was good to see you, too," Buddy said, grinning as he waited for my response.

As I put my wallet back in my pocket, I just looked at him with a confused look on my face.

"That always gets people for a moment," Buddy said, laughing. "At least until they figure out I'm pulling their leg."

Chapter Twelve

I had lunch at the Piccadilly Cafeteria on Congress Avenue before leaving Austin and heading south to San Antonio, where I was to meet with Jerry Don Lane, Kerry Vogel's short-lived UT roommate. Pushing my tray down the serving line at Piccadilly, I had to fight the impulse to get more food than I could possibly eat. By the time I reached the checker I had selected a spring salad with blue cheese dressing, large chopped beef, mashed potatoes with brown gravy, green beans, soft roll, ice water, and iced tea.

When I got to my table, I took my food off the tray and sat down to enjoy it. A friendly waitress in a rust colored uniform came by and picked up the empty tray. I maneuvered the chopped beef in front of me and, in a clockwise manner, arranged the salad, mashed potatoes, green beans and soft roll. I unrolled the utensils and put the napkin in my lap. Tearing off a portion of the soft roll, I sopped up some au jus in the chopped beef plate and ate some. Then I put the blue cheese dressing on the salad and ate a little of it.

Sister Charlene was a real looker according to Buddy Connor. Of course, he was blind. *The blind leading the blind.* Buddy seemed to be a reliable source despite his handicap. Connecting Sister Charlene and the Church of the Chosen to Kerry Vogel eight years ago was a little improbable, but it was the only lead I had at this point, so I decided to go with it. After all, something was telling me I was on the right track.

After lunch I drove to San Antonio and checked into the Marriott on the River Walk. I met Jerry Don Lane in the hotel bar a little past six. It was almost dark and the festive lights of the river walk decorated the early evening. Jerry Don walked up to me at the bar and said, "You Cassidy?"

"That would be me," I said.

"Jerry Don Lane," he said shaking hands.

He looked around as if to see if he knew anyone in the bar and then sat on the barstool next to me. I made a motion to the bartender and he took our order. I asked him to bring me a Heineken with a shot of tequila and Jerry Don requested the same thing, but with a Budweiser.

"I think we just might get along," Jerry Don said. "A man can't be too bad if he's ordering beer and Jose Cuervo."

"What can you tell me about Kerry Vogel?"

"What do you want to know? I only knew him for a short while before he disappeared."

The bartender brought our drinks and Jerry Don and I turned our attention to the tequila and beer. After I took my shot and drank some beer, I looked at Jerry Don who was washing his down with a big gulp of Budweiser.

"Who was this Charlie I keep hearing about?" I said.

"Don't know for sure but I always thought it was some girl."

"Did you tell the police that?"

"I might have mentioned it, but it was a long time ago."

"How did you and Kerry get to be roommates?"

"Coaches decide that," Jerry Don said. "I believe we were assigned to be roomies because of our positions. Quarterbacks and wide receivers often bunk together."

A very pretty waitress in a very tight blouse showing a lot of cleavage, and wearing an equally tight pair of short shorts, walked up and stood at the opening next to Jerry Don and ordered drinks from the bartender. Jerry Don said something to her and she laughed. They talked for a few minutes before the waitress put the drinks on her tray and walked away.

"You know, Cassidy," Jerry Don got the bartender's attention and motioned for another round, "I've heard all about what you did in Fort Worth, but I'm not your next big story."

"I realize that Jerry Don. I'm just trying to find out what happened to Kerry. I'm not here to throw blame on you. I'm just here to find out what he was up to eight years ago. Is there anything you can tell me that will help in our investigation?"

"I'm a banker now, Cassidy. I gotta good job, nice family, and friends who respect me."

"Like I said…just tell me what you can about Kerry."

"Well, it's not much."

"Anything will be helpful."

Jerry Don shrugged.

"Kerry showed up and the first day of practice he was gangbusters. Ran the option to perfection and his passes were razor sharp and on the button."

"That was the first day," I said. "What happened after that?"

"It was like he didn't care anymore."

Jerry Don searched for the bartender hoping the delivery of round two would come soon.

"It was almost eerie," he said. "I passed him on the way out to practice the next several days and he was always on the pay phone in the dorm foyer. When I said anything to him he would turn away talking to someone on the phone in a soft voice."

"Is that when you heard him mention the name 'Charlie'?" I said.

"Yes," Jerry Don said, "and when he got to practice the coaches came down on him hard and everyone knew it was only a matter of time before he got kicked off the team. You can't show up late for practice as many times as he did without being cut. Then one day he never came back and later we heard he disappeared."

"What do you believe happened to Kerry?" I said.

"I think he got mixed up with a woman who messed with his mind," Jerry Don said.

"There are those who say his odd behavior may be due to drugs."

"I don't know who those people are, but they're dead wrong. The coaches didn't allow that kind of stuff to go on with the incoming freshmen."

"Coaches can monitor only so much," I said.

"Well," Jerry Don said, reaching for some cashews in a bowl within reach, "I spent five years with my recruiting class and Kerry is the only one who screwed up."

He tossed a couple of cashews in his mouth.

"Most of us have gone on to have good lives," he said, chewing the cashews, "and Kerry would have, too, if he hadn't vanished."

The bartender brought our second round. Jerry Don picked up his shot glass and held it up in a toasting gesture.

"Here's to you, Kerry Vogel. Wherever in the hell you are."

Chapter Thirteen

Domingo Perez left a message for me at the Holiday Inn on the River. I arrived back in Austin mid-morning and checked back in to what now was beginning to feel like my home-away-from-home. A James Taylor song drifted through my mind.

Here I am again...Holiday Inn...same old four walls again...

The message said he had some new information. After I checked into my new room that looked just like the last one, I drove over to Perez's office at the Travis County Courthouse. He sat behind his desk looking the part of a real life Texas Ranger. His Stetson hung on a hat rack behind him and his dark blue long sleeve shirt was crisply starched. The Texas Ranger badge above his left pocket and the gun belt holstering his shiny Colt .45 semiautomatic was impressive.

We were drinking coffee as I sat opposite him talking about the Church of the Chosen.

"After we talked the other night I used our resources to find out more about that church you mentioned," Perez said, as he shuffled through several folders stacked in front of him.

"What did you find out?"

"They used to have a big church in Houston."

"They don't anymore?"

"Not anymore," Perez said. "Either the well dried up or they found greener pastures elsewhere. They ceased to exist sometime around 1970."

"Does that mean they are no longer around or they set up operations somewhere else?"

"Must be operating in some other state because they were doing very well with membership and fundraising until...," Perez opened a folder and ran his finger down a document. Then he looked up at me and said, "Looks as if they pulled in ten million plus before they left Texas."

"Where did you find out all this?" I said.

"That's what we do, Cassidy. We're Texas Rangers. We investigate."

Perez smiled as if he was the cat that ate the canary.

"You investigate churches?" I said.

"We routinely investigate religious organizations that fall into the category of possible *cults*."

"That might be trying to dupe the public out of hard earned money," I said.

"And not so hard earned money," Perez said.

"Can you tell me where they are now?"

"Sorry...but I can tell you who was listed as the founder and leader of the 'Chosen.'"

"Who would that be?" I said.

Perez looked back at the document.

"His name is Reverend Malachi Jackson. You heard of him?"

"No…is that his real name?"

"That's all we have."

"Is there anything in your files on Sister Charlene?"

"Nothing in here on her," Perez said.

"Malachi Jackson," I said, pronouncing the name slowly.

"*Reverend* Malachi Jackson," Perez said.

"Of course…I don't know what I was thinking. Praise the Lord and pass the soup."

Chapter Fourteen

Kelly left another message at the Holiday Inn on the River. I stuffed the message into the right pocket of my leather jacket and went upstairs. On the way up I grabbed a copy of today's Austin American-Statesman. Sitting on the bed, I flipped through the sections looking for the sports page when something caught my eye above the fold in the local section. A headline read, 'Blind Store Owner Assaulted and Hospitalized.' I pulled the section out and read the story.

"A blind store owner in east Austin was hospitalized Tuesday when unknown assailants entered his place of business and assaulted him causing serious injuries. Maxwell 'Buddy' Connor, 62, was taken to Brackettville Hospital by Travis County Emergency Ambulance where he underwent surgery."

I walked through the front door of Brackettville Hospital less than thirty minutes later. The lady at the information desk directed me to intensive care on the fourth floor. A nurse in a white uniform stood behind a counter at the nurse's station and eyed me as I stepped out of the elevator.

"What can I do for you, sir?" the nurse said.

"I'm here to see Buddy Connor," I said.

"Only family members are allowed to see him," she said. "I suppose *you* are a family member as well?"

"What do you mean by that?" I said, questioning the tone of her voice more than the words she used.

"Two men came by about an hour ago and wanted to see him, too," she said. "When I told them I had to clear it with Mrs. Connor first...they left without saying another word."

"No, I am not family," I said. "But would you let Mrs. Connor know that Pat Cassidy is here and I would like to talk to her."

'Ms. Nurse in the White Uniform' turned around and pushed a button on the intercom system behind her and said, "Mrs. Connor."

A small, shaky voice said through a speaker, "Yes."

"A gentleman by the name of Pat Cassidy is here at the nurse's station and would like to talk to you."

"All right," Mrs. Connor said. "I'll be right there."

Mrs. Connor came out of the first room to my left at the end of the nurse's station. She was of slender build with a gaunt face that showed the hardships in her past. The dark circles around her brown eyes were framed by long stringy silver hair.

"I'm Mildred Connor," she said, looking at me and then at the nurse for reinforcement.

"I'm Pat Cassidy."

She didn't seem to have the strength to shake hands so I didn't even try.

"My husband told me about your visit the other day," Mrs. Connor said. "He was so excited about it…and now this has happened to him."

Her facial expression remained the same as she spoke with a wearisome voice.

"May I buy you a cup of coffee?" I said.

"Yes," she said, "that would be nice. We can go to the cafeteria downstairs."

Mrs. Connor walked to the elevator without saying anything else and stood in front of the door. I followed her and pushed the down button on the elevator and we waited side by side for the door to open. In the hospital cafeteria, she sat across the table sipping coffee, looking at me with a blank stare.

"Will I be able to talk to Buddy?" I asked.

"He'll be out for awhile," she said. "Right now the doctors have him heavily sedated."

"Was he able to tell you what happened?"

"On the way to the hospital in the ambulance," she said. "Buddy regained consciousness and told me two men came into the store and started pushing him around. They dragged him into the living room and started hitting him."

"How bad are his injuries?"

"Buddy has a concussion, two broken ribs, a dislocated shoulder, and…," Mrs. Connor stopped. Her bottom lip quivered and her eyes filled with tears, "…his face is all swollen and bruised. I could hardly recognize him."

"Did he know who the men were?"

"He didn't say, Mr. Cassidy. After all, as you know, he's blind."

"Please, call me Pat."

Mrs. Connor nodded.

"The past fifteen years have been so hard on us. You know, since Buddy lost his sight. The bank took away our farm near Bastrop after that cow kicked him in the head and he couldn't work anymore. I had to get a job working in a factory and we started the store just to give Buddy something to do. I just don't know how we're going to pay for the hospital bill. We can't afford health insurance and we don't have any money."

"Mrs. Connor," I said, "I believe this has something to do with a case I'm working on right now."

"What makes you think that, Pat?"

"I don't want to go into it right now, but my boss is good for the hospital bill. He'll take care of it."

Suddenly her eyes brightened and she smiled ever so faintly.

"Thank you and God bless you, son."

"I want to talk to Buddy when he comes around," I said.

"By the way, Pat," she said. "Call me Mildred. Would you mind coming back upstairs and sitting with me until he comes out of it?"

"It would be my pleasure."

Chapter Fifteen

Mildred slept in a chair next to Buddy's bed. I sat in a chair in the corner reading an article in a popular sports magazine about the four teams in the finals of the NCAA Basketball Tournament. It was rather anticlimactic, since I already knew that Indiana won the championship last week over Michigan. Bobby Knight got his first title as a coach and the Hoosiers won their third. Buddy's face was contorted and blue around the eyes and cheek bones. His upper body was taped and bandaged. The curtains were pulled back and nightfall had ushered in the bright lights of Austin. I leaned my head back against the high backed chair and wondered why Buddy, of all people, had gotten pulled into the odd disappearance of Kerry Vogel. Looking over at him, I noticed a slight movement of his head. Then Buddy began abruptly jerking his head from side to side making a low groaning sound.

"Stop!" he said through split and swollen lips. "Stop…please don't hit me anymore!"

Mildred bolted from her chair to his bedside and grabbed Buddy's right hand.

"I'm here, Buddy," she said. "It's O.K. I'm here."

Buddy seemed to calm with the sound of his wife's voice and the touch of her hands.

"You're in the hospital," Mildred said. "You're safe now and Pat Cassidy is here to see you."

"Pat is here?" Buddy said, raising his head toward his wife's voice.

Mildred kissed his forehead and then looked at me.

"I'm right here, Buddy," I said.

Turning his head toward me, Buddy said, "Pat, some bad men warned me they would kill you if you don't stop looking for the 'Chosen.' They beat me up to send you a message. They told me to tell you that they would kill you and anyone else that came looking for them."

"Is there anything you can tell me about them? The sound of their voices, how they smelled…anything?"

Buddy's bloodshot eyes focused on my face, and as he had done in his store, peered at me as if he could see me.

"They smelled like dirty clothes and B.O. They were Mexican. Their English was as bad as their body odor and they were mean. I thought…," Buddy began to cry, "…they were going to cut my throat."

"That's enough, Buddy," Mrs. Connor said. "Nothing is going to happen to you now. You rest and let me take care of everything."

"Buddy," I said. "Those men won't be coming back again. If they do, we'll catch them. I'm going to call a friend of mine and have a policeman posted outside your door to keep you safe."

"You can do that, Pat?" Mildred said.

"It's a phone call away," I said.

Buddy slowly closed his eyes and drifted off again into a deep sleep.

I called Domingo Perez and he arranged for several off duty Austin Police officers to alternate shifts outside of Buddy's hospital room for the next several days. Of course, as Dad would say, it was on Jeb's nickel. At nine-thirty a Candy Striper came to the door and motioned me into the hallway. Mildred was asleep in the corner chair and Buddy rested quietly in his bed.

"A police officer is at the nurse's station," the Candy Striper said, pointing toward the station. "He wants to talk to you."

The Austin Police Officer in full dark blue uniform greeted me in front of 'Ms. Nurse in a White Uniform.' She seemed to be impressed as we shook hands.

"Officer Trent Billingsly, Mr. Cassidy," he said.

"Call me Pat. Is it O.K. if I call you Trent?"

He nodded.

"We'll be here according to your wishes," Trent said.

"Around the clock, Trent, until Mr. Connor goes home."

"Yes, sir," he said.

"Thanks."

"Pat, what's this all about?"

"I'm not sure, but don't let anyone get near him that isn't approved by either his wife or me. Mr. Connor has been severely beaten and may still be in danger. I want him protected."

"No one will," Trent said, "you have my word."

"That's good enough for me," I said.

Trent made his way to Buddy's room and went inside. 'Ms. Nurse in a White Uniform' sent the Candy Striper in the other direction to check on a patient in room 415.

"Excuse me, ma'am," I said to the nurse. "Earlier I didn't have a chance to introduce myself properly. My name is Pat Cassidy."

"I remember your name," she said. "But, who are you?"

"I'm…ah…," I paused, trying to think of a way to describe to her who I am. Finally I said, "I'm looking into the disappearance of a young man from Brownwood."

"Are you a private investigator?"

"No, you have to have a license to be a private investigator. I work for Jeb Glasscock's Corporation as a troubleshooter."

"You mean the billionaire Jeb Glasscock?"

"Yes,' I said.

"Well, you should have said so. I'm Betty Ruth Henry," she said, looking down for her nametag.

She pulled back her pink sweater that was concealing the nametag and pointed at it. The nametag read, "Betty R. Henry, LVN."

"Oh, where are my manners?" Nurse Henry reached over the counter to shake hands.

"May I ask you a few questions about the men that were here earlier today trying to see Mr. Connor?" I said.

"Sure, it appears you're O.K. since Mrs. Connor is treating you like family," Nurse Henry said, "*and* you've gotten the Austin P.D here to protect Mr. Conner. What would you like to know?"

"What did the two men look like?"

"Like they don't belong around here…that's for sure."

"Can you describe them?"

"They were tall, hard lookin' men," she said. "Dirty lookin' men…the kind you wouldn't want to run into in a dark alley. They were Mexican. I mean they were from Mexico. I grew up in Laredo and I know a Mexican when I see one…and in this case…hear one. Their accent was as thick as thieves."

"Was there anything else about them that stood out?" I said.

"Yeah, now that you mention it…they had a peculiar smell. Like a cross between cabbage cooking and…" Nurse Henry made a circling motion with her right hand.

"Body odor?" I said.

"Yes!" she said. "That's it! I had to spray room freshener to cover up the smell they left behind."

Billingsly came out of Buddy's room with a chair in his hand and put it down beside the door. He nodded at me and sat down in the chair.

"Mr. Cassidy," Nurse Henry said, "do you think those men are the same men that assaulted Mr. Connor?"

"Yes I do," I said.

"Then, you better be careful…the look in their eyes sent a chill down my spine. It was like looking into the eyes of men without a soul."

Chapter Sixteen

Exhausted from worry and lack of sleep, Mildred left the care of Buddy to the medical staff and went home to sleep in her own bed. Buddy's safety was now up to off-duty Austin Police Officer Trent Billingsly, as I called it a night and stepped into the elevator to go down to my car. A sleepy-eyed doctor in blue scrubs greeted me on the way out of the emergency room sliding door. When I arrived earlier in the day the parking lot was full. Now my car sat alone across the empty parking lot facing Red River Street. Dull blue light illuminated the outside of the hospital from mercury vapor lights scattered throughout the parking area. After the events of the day, I wasn't totally surprised to see two men on each side of my car as if they were up to no good. The man on the driver's side had a red bandana around his head and was down on one knee opening up a suitcase. The other man was peeking into the passenger side window. I pulled out my gun, loaded a round into the chamber and walked slowly toward them with the Browning pointed at the ground. The clunking sound of my boots gave me away halfway across the parking lot. 'Bandana' stood up with a gun in his hand, took a shot at me, and missed. Still walking toward him, I raised the Browning and fired off a round that struck him in the shoulder causing him to drop his weapon. The other man disappeared into the bushes that separated the parking lot and sidewalk from the street. The shooter was a very tall, solid looking Hispanic. As I walked up to him, I saw that blood covered the hand he was using to cover his shoulder.

"Arturo," 'Bandana' said with an icy stare, "¡Mátalo!"

From the corner of my eye I saw Arturo rise up from the bushes and level a semiautomatic at me. I quickly reacted and shot him in the chest, sending him into a backward spin and out of sight. All of a sudden 'Bandana' body-blocked me to the ground. He picked his revolver up off the pavement while I was still on the ground and ran through the bushes. 'Bandana' was in the middle of the street dodging traffic by the time I got back on my feet. A car blew its horn and skidded to an abrupt stop just missing him. He was headed for Waterloo Park across the street. I knew if he made it across Waller Creek I might lose him in the thickly wooded area. I chased after 'Bandana' as fast as I could with my nine millimeter in my right hand. He ran with a slight limp as he entered the park. I knew at this rate I would eventually overtake him, but I also knew the creek was less than a hundred yards away. Running past the park entrance, I saw 'Bandana' turn and look back at me. When he turned around he bulldozed over an elderly homeless woman and her shopping cart. The woman fell hard to the sidewalk and the shopping cart spilled its contents onto the ground as 'Bandana' shoulder rolled over both of them and came up running. Once I hurdled over the shopping cart, the distance between us was only a few yards. Then he disappeared into the shadowy darkness of a cluster of trees. I stopped to let my eyes adjust to the darkness, when I saw a flash and then heard the sound of a gunshot as a bullet whizzed through the air. I hit the ground as six more shots rang out. Then I heard the clicking sound of 'Bandana's' empty revolver and his footsteps splashing into Waller Creek. Flashing lights and sirens from Austin P.D. patrol cars ripped through the darkness from all directions. My eyes were focused now, and with the additional light from the headlights, I could see 'Bandana' lumbering down the creek. The spray of light from a squad car approaching from the opposite side of the park lit up a path through the cluster of trees. I stuffed my gun in its holster and sprinted through the woods arriving at the creek the same time 'Bandana' passed in front of me. Leaping into the air, we collided and fell onto the bank on the other side of the narrow stream. 'Bandana' was exhausted and lay on the ground gasping for air.

"I think you've finally met your Waterloo," I said, pulling out my gun and pointing it at him.

Chapter Seventeen

Domingo Perez stood next to his former partner at the Austin P.D., Detective Jack McKay. Perez was wearing a black Texas Department of Public Safety baseball cap with white DPS letters on the front, a yellow polo shirt tucked into his blue jeans, tennis shoes, badge, and a holstered Colt .45. McKay was taller than Perez and dressed as if he just came from the office.

"I was about to go home when I got the call," McKay said.

"Cassidy's working on one of our cold cases," Perez said.

Perez sniffed the cool night air and coughed.

"The officers first on the scene told me you were very cooperative," McKay said.

"I was," I said. "I put my gun down on the ground, hands over my head, identified myself, and warned them 'Bandana' was dangerous."

"He's one bad Mexican," McKay said. "He kicked the hell out of one of my officers when he tried to put him in the squad car."

McKay held a light overcoat draped over his right forearm. His knit black tie was loose at the collar and his white long sleeve dress shirt was rolled up and reflected the red and blue flashing lights from the police cars that surrounded us. A .38 caliber was strapped in a brown leather holster on his right hip. McKay's lanky stature drooped and his eyes were tired.

"How in the hell did you apprehend this guy?" McKay said.

"I ran him into the ground, which wasn't difficult since he had a bullet hole in his shoulder."

"Well…the paramedics took care of that."

McKay checked over his shoulder to see if 'Bandana' was still under control. He sat handcuffed in the back of a squad car.

"Does he speak English?" I said.

"Very little," McKay said, "that's where my 'Spic' former partner comes into play."

"Hey," Perez said. "If it wasn't for me, your sorry 'Mick' ass would still be writing traffic tickets."

"Keep on dreamin', Perez," McKay said.

"I want to be present when you question him," I said.

"Which cold case are you working on?" McKay said.

"Kerry Vogel."

"Oh, yeah," McKay said, "the kid who disappeared back in '68."

"Cassidy's made a connection," Perez said, "between a religious group called the Church of the Chosen and the kid's disappearance."

"What in the hell does this slimeball have to do with a religious group?" McKay said.

"Exactly what I would like to know," I said.

"I'd put my money on'em being a Mexican drug runner," Perez said.

A uniformed Austin Police Officer walked up and said, "Lieutenant, the other shooter is dead. He took one in the heart."

McKay glanced at me and then back at the officer.

"Go on," he said.

"No I.D. of course. It appears Mr. Cassidy interrupted their plans to wire his car with a bomb."

McKay, Perez, and the officer all looked at me, but there was no emotion on my face.

"The bomb squad is on the way," the officer continued. "The man apprehended by Mr. Cassidy emptied an eight shot Smith & Wesson .357 Magnum. We found it on the trail leading to the creek."

"Expensive toy for a Mexican," Perez said with amusement.

"How about the woman he knocked down?" I said.

"She's O.K.," the officer said. "She was worried more about the contents of her shopping cart than she was with the bruise on her forehead."

"Well, let's go talk to this scumbag and find out what we can," McKay said.

"This should be interesting," I said.

Chapter Eighteen

Austin's nightlife beckoned as I pulled out of the parking lot of the police department. Texas Ranger Domingo Perez and Lieutenant Jack McKay interrogated 'Bandana' for over two hours. McKay permitted me to sit in on the interrogation, but all they were able to get out of him was his name, if it really was his name. 'Bandana' told Perez, who acted as the interpreter, that his name was Gorge Ortega Ortiz Delgado. The stop light at Eighth Street and Nueces changed to red, so I slowed the Malibu to a complete stop and thought about the acronym the letters of his name spelled. *G.O.O.D.? This man is anything but good.* Delgado's lawyer waltzed into the Austin P.D. about midnight to begin the process of posting his bail. The lawyer had flown in from Houston on a moment's notice, and according to Perez and McKay, had a reputation for representing Mexican drug cartels.

It appears the gyre is widening.

"I'm Pat Cassidy," I said to the man behind the desk at the Holiday Inn on the River. "Do I have any messages?"

"Yes, you do, Mr. Cassidy," as he checked the slots on the wall behind him and handed me a slip of paper.

The message was from UT assistant football coach, Mike Earl. "Call me ASAP," the message said.

I looked at my watch. It was almost one o'clock in the morning. Considering the time of night, I put off returning his call until first thing in the morning.

The barstools were empty in the hotel bar as I pulled up a stool and ordered a Heineken and tequila. The bartender was a handsome, broad shouldered man with a mustache, and a healthy head of brown hair. He wore a ruffled white shirt, black vest, and black slacks. The barroom was spattered with a dozen or so patrons and a lone waitress standing in front of the juke box selecting songs to play. She was wearing a similar outfit. Instead of black slacks, however, she had on a short black skirt that was pleasant to see.

"Beer and tequila," the bartender said, as he sat them in front of me.

The bartender stood watching me as I drank the tequila and washed it down with the beer.

"Feel better?" he said.

"I will in a few seconds," I said.

"Have a hard day?" he asked.

I grinned at him and took another swig of beer.

"I guess not," he said, grinning back. "My name's Rick."

"Pat Cassidy," I said.

"I thought you looked familiar," Rick said.

"Yeah...I know," I said. "The Calloway thing made a lot of news last month."

Rick picked up a lime and began slicing it into sections on a cutting board.

"I take it," he said, "you aren't comfortable with all the notoriety."

"I was just trying to right a huge wrong. My best friend was murdered."

He nodded.

"What brings you to Austin?" Rick said, trimming the edges of the lime slices.

The juke box played 'A Legend in My Time' by Ronnie Milsap. The waitress took drink orders from a table in the middle of the barroom and I noticed how nice her legs looked in black fishnet hose.

"Looking for a missing person," I said.

"Anyone I know?" Rick said.

"I doubt it," I said, finishing off the beer.

"Try me," Rick said. "I'm more than just a bartender."

"Eight years ago a kid from Brownwood disappeared while going through two-a-days at UT."

"You're right," Rick said. "My wife and I only moved here four years ago. We came down here from Michigan. She got a real good job as one of the brainiacs at Texas Instruments."

"What about you?" I said. "What's your day job?"

"I sell drugs," Rick said, laughing.

I smiled at him trying not to look shocked by his comment.

He looked up from the slicing, and said, "I'm a pharmaceutical salesman."

Pointing at him with my index finger, I said, "You got me."

"That always gets them," Rick said. "Want another round?"

"Sure."

Rick served me up another round of beer and tequila.

"So, Pat," Rick said, "I hear you're a radio sportscaster."

"I am," I said, enjoying another shot of tequila.

"Then…why are you in Austin looking for a missing person?"

"Beats the hell out of me," I said.

Chapter Nineteen

The ringing of the telephone woke me up the next morning. It was a wakeup call for an early morning run that was long overdue. A few minutes later I was stretching in front of the Holiday Inn wearing a t-shirt, shorts, and running shoes. The run up East Avenue took me to First Street where I turned west and picked up the pace for about a mile before turning south on Lamar Boulevard. A quarter-of-a-mile later, I jogged east on Barton Springs Road watching the sun rise on the horizon. The traffic paid little attention to me as I made my way over the Colorado River on Congress Avenue Bridge. I jogged across First Street, past the State Capitol Building, up to Sixth Street, over to Trinity, across First Street again, and finally to East Avenue which took me back to my starting point at the motel. Walking around the outside of the Holiday Inn to cool down, I tried to figure out how far the run had been. The way I was sweating and the rate of my breathing told me it was close to five miles.

Once showered and shaved, I had breakfast in the hotel restaurant. At eight o'clock I returned to my room and called Mike Earl.

"Yeah, Cassidy, I was talking to Coach King the other day about our visit."

"Yeah...," I said.

"Well...to make a long story short, he wants to talk to you. We're having Spring Drills and we'll be out on the field in about an hour. Think you can come by and see him?"

"I'll see you in an hour," I said.

Darrell King was standing on the sideline at Memorial Stadium watching his coaching staff lead the Longhorn football team in drills. He was easy to spot as I entered the stadium through the south gate. King wore sunglasses with his coaching uniform that consisted of a burnt orange cap with a white 'T', 'LONGHORNS' written across the chest of a white t-shirt in burnt orange letters and burnt orange coaching shorts. He held a whistle in his right hand as if he was ready to blow it.

"How ya doin'?" King said, as I walked up to him.

We shook hands.

"Pat Cassidy," I said.

"Glad to meet you, Pat."

King took his right hand and pushed the bill of his cap upward until it rested high upon on his head.

"When you were in the coach's office the other day I thought to myself, 'I think I need to talk to that young man.' Hell, I didn't know why at the time, but after talking to Mike, I put two and two together and figured it out."

"So what do you have on Kerry Vogel?"

"Kerry Vogel," King said. "Now there's a name that just won't go away. One of our biggest disappointments…what happened to him is a real unsolved mystery."

"It's an unsolved mystery I'm trying to solve," I said.

"That's what Mike was telling me."

King pulled off his cap and ran his free hand over his black hair and repositioned the cap on top of his head.

"I'd like to help if I can," King said, "so, if you have any questions for me…then ask away."

"Thanks, Coach, I appreciate it. In fact, I do have some questions that I would like to ask."

"Let me hear them," King said.

"Do the names Rev. Malachi Jackson, Sister Charlene or The Church of the Chosen ring a bell?"

"Never heard of the church, but what were those names again?"

"Rev. Malachi Jackson and Sister Charlene."

"You know," King said, "I had a report from campus security of a woman named Sister 'something or other' wandering around outside the stadium back then, but I never gave it much thought."

"What did campus security actually say?" I said.

"The best I can remember they said a pretty blonde with a name similar to…," King paused, "what did you say her name was?"

"Sister Charlene."

"Yeah, that was it. They said she was walking around the stadium handing out some kind of weird religious material."

"Is there any kind of a record of that report?" I said.

"I don't think so," King said. "Stadium security back then consisted of Jerry Slovak and he died last year. Jerry never kept records. If he saw anything out of the ordinary he just reported it to me."

"Well, believe it or not, this helps a lot."

"Glad I could help," King said.

"By the way," King said. "Tell Jeb Glasscock we appreciate his financial support. You know he's one of our biggest contributors don't you?"

"It doesn't surprise me one little bit."

Chapter Twenty

My suitcase, briefcase, and leather jacket sat on the end of the bed waiting for me to load up and head out to Brownwood. Sitting by the telephone, I readjusted the shoulder strap of my holster to make the Browning in it fit snugly underneath my left arm. A yellow legal pad sat on the table next to the bed underneath the lamp. Written on it was a time line of the week's activities in chronological order. The only thing I knew when I arrived on Tuesday was that Kerry Vogel disappeared in 1968. Four days later, through a stroke of luck, the investigation has turned up a connection between Kerry and The Church of the Chosen, who themselves up and left Texas not long after Kerry vanished. Now, we apparently have a connection between the 'Chosen' and Mexican drug runners, who had no qualms about beating up a defenseless blind man and blowing people up.

I had pretty well exhausted all my excuses for not returning Kelly's phone calls. She had called me twice and left a message to call her back each time. I hadn't yet, but since I wasn't one to shirk a responsibility, I gave in and dialed her number.

"Hello," a man's voice said.

Somewhat surprised Kelly didn't answer, I started to hang up. I knew I had dialed the correct number.

"May I speak with Kelly?"

Silence on the other end of the line. A few moments later Kelly spoke.

"Hi, Pat," she said in a voice that was noncommittal.

"I'm returning your calls," I said.

"It took you long enough."

"Well, after the other night, I think I would be justified if I never called you back.

"Don't be such a big baby, Pat."

Silence on my end. My father always tried to tell me I should think about what I was going to say before I said it, especially when I was pissed off at someone. His life's lessons were beginning to sink in.

"Are you there?" Kelly said.

"Yes," I said.

"Are you mad at me?"

"Disappointed."

"In me?" she asked.

"Yes."

"Are you disappointed because I left with Larry the other night?"

"Yes," I said, again.

"What forever for?" Kelly said. "You hurt him really bad, Pat. Someone had to take care of him."

"He didn't look that hurt to me."

"Well, he was."

"Kelly, you've been telling me you think there is something going on between us and just when I was about to take you seriously…you up and run off with your old boyfriend."

"Larry needed me. He still needs me. I can't just cut him off again right now."

"Kelly…you can't have your cake and eat it, too."

"What's that supposed to mean?"

"It means you can't have me *and* Larry."

"You need to give me more time."

"I can't make any guarantees."

Kelly didn't say anything for a few seconds. Larry's voice whispered in the background.

"How is your eye?" Kelly said.

"It's fine. Larry doesn't have much of a punch."

"Call me, O.K.?" Kelly said. "I graduate in a month. You are coming to my graduation?"

"We'll see, Kelly," I said, and hung up without saying another word.

Chapter Twenty-one

The drive from Austin put me in Brownwood a little before two o'clock in the afternoon. I parked alongside the Brown County Sheriff's Department and went inside. Annie, in full uniform and in fine form, greeted me at the front desk when I came through the door.

"Hi, Pat," she said. "You here to see Sheriff Vogel?"

"Yes, I am."

"Have a seat while I buzz him," Annie said, cranking out a number on her phone. A moment later she said, "Sheriff, Pat Cassidy is here to see you."

Annie had a pretty face and bright-white smile. Her long, straight black hair was pulled back in a tight ponytail. The uniform was fresh and creased, passing my inspection. It did little to hide her femininity.

"Annie," I said. "You went to high school with Kerry Vogel from what I understand."

"I did," she said. "He was two years older than me."

"What can you tell me about him? What was he like in high school?"

Annie looked at me and smiled as a blush filled her light complexion.

"I had a huge crush on Kerry when I was a sophomore."

"Did you ever go out with him?"

"No," Annie said. "Kerry was always nice to me, but he dated the real pretty girls."

"There were more beautiful girls than you in high school?"

Annie looked at me and the blush on her face deepened in color.

"I have improved with maturity."

"Would you characterize Kerry as a nice boy?"

"Oh yes," she said. "All the girls he ever dated said he was so nice."

"But he was a partier from what I'm told."

"Pat, we all liked to party, but Kerry wasn't a drunk or pothead. Kerry was always in control whether he was on the football field, in the classroom, or in a social setting."

"So, what are you saying?"

"I'm saying," Annie paused for a moment, and then said, "Kerry wasn't perfect, but he had a quality about him that you couldn't help but love."

Annie turned on her electric typewriter and the IBM Selectric spun around and came to attention. She then fed a police form into the carriage and rolled it to the right spot and flipped down the paper bar.

"Kerry had an air about him...like he was destined for something."

"What did you think his destiny was going to be?"

"I always thought Kerry would spend his life protecting others, maybe like some kind of cop."

"Interesting," I said. "Why would you say that?"

"Kerry liked to protect people. He didn't allow any of his football buddies to bully anyone."

"Kerry could do that?"

"Yes, he could...everyone respected him, and with J.T. as his backup, no one ever questioned their intentions."

"J.T. does make great backup," I said.

Annie nodded.

"Were Kerry's intentions always altruistic?"

"You mean were they always honorable?"

"Yes."

"Most of the time they were. Kerry was a nice boy, but he was tough."

"Does everyone from high school remember Kerry as fondly as you do?"

"Well...," Annie said, grinning. "Most of the girls do."

Chapter Twenty-two

"So, what have you come up with in Austin?" Sheriff Vogel said, sitting behind his desk.

"I believe I've found a connection between Kerry and a woman named Charlene. Her name is Sister Charlene to be more exact."

I stood in front of his desk waiting for an invitation to sit down.

Vogel sat with his legs crossed, hands clasped together in his lap, and twiddling his thumbs. He stood up and walked to the corner of his office and peered at a watercolor painting on the wall of a windmill on the plains at sunset.

"What kind of name is that?" Vogel said. "Sounds like some kind of hippie singing group."

"Not quite," I said.

"What, then?" Vogel snapped back at me.

The Sheriff shook his head and then moved his neck in a circular motion trying to relax the tension he was feeling.

"I'm sorry, Pat. Hell, have a seat. It's just been a hard week."

Sitting down in a chair in front of his desk, I studied the Sheriff's demeanor as he returned his attention to the painting. He looked annoyed more than he seemed tired. Vogel looked at the picture again, as if to vent the tension gnawing at him, and then sat down in his chair.

"I apologize for being so short with you," Vogel said. "I've always been a little edgy when it comes to finding out the truth about Kerry. So, tell me about this Sister Charlene."

"She was with a religious cult known as the Church of the Chosen," I said.

"What's the connection?"

"I'll get there," I said. "The Church of the Chosen was having a revival the week Kerry disappeared, and Sister Charlene was seen handing out religious material outside Memorial Stadium…presumably right about the same time your son would have been coming or going to practice."

Vogel nodded and shifted slightly in his chair.

"Reports from the police and his roommate have him talking on the phone to someone he called 'Charlie' a few days before he disappeared."

Vogel picked up a pen and wrote down Sister Charlene's name on a yellow legal pad on his desk, and said, "I remember Detective Perez telling me that when I was looking for him back then."

"Perez was very helpful. He's a Texas Ranger now."

Vogel signaled with a slight dip of his head.

"How 'bout McKay?" Vogel said. "Is he still…"

"Still there…still a detective," I said. "There is more to the story, Sheriff. I questioned a blind store owner down the street from where The Church of the Chosen used to be located and found out they packed up and left town right after Kerry's disappearance. Here's the kicker…the day after I talked to the store owner…two thugs show up and beat him to within an inch of his life."

"You think it was a coincidence?" Vogel said.

"It wasn't a coincidence," I said. "The blind man, Buddy Connor, was hospitalized. I went to see him as soon as I found out about the beating and when I left the hospital that night; I interrupted a couple of thugs trying to plant a bomb in my car."

Vogel glanced up at me with renewed interest and I told him the rest of the story.

"What are you going to do now?"

"Send J.T. to Houston to see what he can find out about these people," I said. "The Church of the Chosen operated out of Houston until about 1970. I'd go myself, but I need to be back in Fort Worth on Monday to take care of a few things."

Vogel nodded.

"Pat," Vogel said, leaning forward placing his elbows on his desk with his hands under his chin, "I don't know how to tell you this, but I guess I need to."

"J.T. changed his mind," I said.

"Yes, but I'll let him tell you why. I hired a deputy from Erath County to take his place, but fortunately, the commissioners are going to let me keep him *and* J.T."

"Meaning?"

"You can have J.T. to help you find Kerry."

"Thanks, I'll need him."

"I know you will," Vogel said. "J.T. is an excellent cop."

Chapter Twenty-three

When I walked out of Vogel's office, J.T. was sitting in the same chair I had sat in earlier while talking with Annie.

"Let's take a drive," J.T. said, standing up and putting on a new Resistol straw cowboy hat.

J.T. drove us out of town on County Road 279 toward Lake Brownwood. During the drive I told him in detail everything that had happened in Austin. Near a pavilion at Shamrock Shores, we leaned against the hood of his Brown County Sheriff's Department unit looking across the lake. Bluebonnets covered the hillside that sloped down to the water's edge and the breeze off the lake was cool underneath the shade of a large pecan tree.

"So, that brings us back to you," I said. "You in or out of this thing with me?"

"This is home, Pat."

"That the only reason?"

"I like my job here," J.T. said. "In Brownwood I'm somebody important to the people."

"You're important to Jeb…and you're important to me."

"I appreciate that, but moving to Fort Worth just doesn't feel right at this point in my life."

The wind picked up and the rustling pecan trees announced its arrival. J.T. repositioned his new Resistol. The lake became choppy and a passing boat bounced on the waves as it sped toward an unknown destination.

"What if you didn't have to move?"

"You mean you'd set up the office here?"

"Jeb wants me to," I said.

"I don't know, Pat. Sheriff Vogel relies on me a lot, and like I said...I like my job."

"Just think about it. That's all I ask."

"I'm gonna help you find Kerry, but after that I don't know how much help I can be to you."

We both turned our faces to the wind as it changed directions again. The air was fresh and the sky was a clear blue. The kind of blue found only on the Edwards Plateau.

After a while, J.T. said, "I'll think about it."

"I need you to go to Houston and find out as much as you can about the Church of the Chosen."

"Monday soon enough?"

"Yeah," I said. "There are some things I need to take care of in Fort Worth but I think we're headed in the right direction. I'm sure the 'Chosen' has something to do with Kerry's disappearance."

"I'll find out what I can."

"Oh…and be careful. These people are more than just holy-rollers. I'm not sure what the connection is with the men who were trying to blow me up, but whatever it is…it isn't good."

J.T. slowly turned his head and grinned, "Good as in Gorge Ortegaaaa…what were the other two names?"

"Ortiz Delgado…Gorge Ortega Ortiz Delgado," I said, grinning back. "Watch your back…that's all I'm trying to say."

"My friend and I," J.T. said, patting his .44 Magnum holstered to his right hip, "will be just fine."

"I'm impressed," I said. "A real honest-to-goodness tough guy that is grammatically correct."

"It's taken a lifetime of my mother correcting my grammar and four years of college to get that way."

"Every little bit helps."

"I want you to do something for me, Pat."

"What's that?"

"I want you to go see Claire."

"Why?"

"I saw her the other day and she asked about you."

"I should go see her because she asked about me?"

J.T. slid his sunglasses down on the end of his nose and looked at me with a smile.

"Pat, she's a nice lady and you slept with her and never called her again."

"I've been a little busy, J.T."

"You haven't been too busy to call her. All you have to do is pick up the phone and dial."

"I thought calling her would be a little embarrassing for her."

"Why would you think that?"

"She was supposed to be my alibi when I was arrested for the triple murder out at Bobby Ellison's place."

"Claire just told the truth."

"I'm guessing word got around that we were together that night."

"Just slightly," J.T. said.

"I should go see her, huh?"

"Why don't you take her out?"

"I should take her out?"

"Yes, and treat her like the lady she is."

"How 'bout if I just go see her?"

"That would be a start."

Chapter Twenty-four

Western Heights Elementary was located a half a block off Austin Avenue on Idlewild Drive. The brown brick building featured a pattern of interspaced wide windows on each side of a white rock entrance. Old Glory hung at the top of the flagpole flapping in the wind. Claire's light blue Chevrolet Impala was still in the faculty parking lot, so I pulled up along the curb in front of the school and parked.

The office was just inside the front door. The closed dark wood office door had six glass panels allowing me to see inside, where a middle-aged woman with a stiff out-of-date bouffant hairdo stood behind a counter. She had jet black hair, bright red lipstick, a lot of makeup and wore a tight green dress around a voluptuous figure. When she saw me she stopped counting the money in her hand, smiled, and waved at me to come in.

"Hi," I said, opening the door.

"Well look who just walked in…if it's not the man of my dreams."

Smiling at her, I said, "I'm here to see Claire Fleming."

"Just my luck," she said, looking at the money in her hands. "Now see what you've made me do. I've lost count."

"I'm sorry."

"That's alright, darlin'. It was well worth the tingle if you know what I mean."

I couldn't help but smile at the expression she made rolling her eyes upward with a quivering motion.

"Claire Fleming," I repeated. "Can you point me in the direction of her classroom?"

"Oh…of course…you're here to see Miss Fleming. Where are my manners? I'm Betty Walker, school secretary."

Betty put the money down and we shook hands.

"What's your name, handsome?"

Blush filled my face and I was somewhat hesitant and embarrassed to tell her my name.

"Pat Cassidy," I finally decided to say.

"Oh…my goodness…have we heard about you," Betty said with a loud voice. "You scandalous devil you."

"Claire Fleming?" I said a little annoyed.

Betty had something else to say, but thought better of it, as she read my expression. *'Mr. Nice Guy' had left the building.*

"Let me put this money up in my desk and I'll take you down to her room."

Betty grabbed up the cash and put it into a money bag, then locked it in her desk a few feet behind the counter. "Follow me, honey."

The hallway leading to Claire's room was painted rich maroon with occasional white trim. Our footsteps reverberated in the corridor as we passed a series of second grade classrooms on the way to the first grade area at the end of the hall. The doorways featured bright colorful cutouts of animals, clouds, children reading, playing, and laughing. The custodian, a Mexican woman about sixty with gray hair and a tired face, nodded as she passed us sweeping the floor with a push broom.

Claire was straightening desks when we reached her room.

"Miss Fleming," Betty said, prancing inside. "Look what I've got for you. If you don't want him, then send him on back my way."

Betty winked at both of us then prissed out the door and back up the hallway toward the office. Claire had a slight smile on her face, but didn't say anything right away. Her blonde hair was pulled back in a ponytail and she wore a navy blue button up blouse with a round collar and sleeves that curved at the elbows. The tan skirt fit snug at her hips and stopped just above her knees. A small diamond teardrop necklace accented her delicate neckline and she wore very little makeup.

"How have you been?" I asked.

"I'm fine, Pat. Glad to see you're still in one piece."

She returned to straightening the desks where upon reaching the end of a row turned around and drafted a smile making the uneasiness in the room more palatable.

"You're lucky you made it this far," Claire said. "Betty looked like she was about to eat you alive."

"She looks like she could wear a man out."

"She can…or at least that's what I hear." A little of Claire's real personality began to infiltrate the awkwardness of the moment. "So what brings you back to Brownwood?"

"Jeb wants to talk to me about some things."

"Oh," she said as if I had said the wrong thing.

I don't believe that's what she wanted to hear.

Claire walked to her desk and ignored me while she stuffed a stack of papers inside a carrying bag. She then placed a navy blue clutch purse next to it.

"Listen, Pat. Unless you have something to say, I need to go. It's been a long day."

A flush of color changed her complexion as she put the strap of the bag over her right shoulder.

"I came here to ask you out tonight," I said.

Claire let the straps of the bag slide off her arm and it flopped back on top of the desk.

"You did."

I think that put me back on track.

"Yes, I did."

"I don't think I'm ready to go out in public with you right now," Claire said, with the straps of the bag wrapped around her hands.

"Why?" I said, surprised.

"Have you not heard about the talk going on around town about us?"

"J.T. said something about it earlier," I said, "but people are always going to talk."

"Spoken like a man who has never lived in a small town before," Claire bantered.

"Excuse me," I bantered back. "I lived in Brownwood for an entire week."

"That doesn't count, Pat, and you know it. I have to live here," Claire said. "You don't."

"So you're saying if you go out with a guy, people are going to *assume* you sleep with him?"

"No, Pat, they don't, but people already know we spent the night together. Remember, I was supposed to be your alibi."

"O.K., Claire," I said, holding the palms of my hands up in the air. "I'll just be on my way."

The look in Claire's blue eyes didn't match the words that were coming out of her mouth. I could tell she wanted to spend time with me, but I didn't want to make a scene in her classroom. I turned around to leave.

"Don't go, Pat."

Turning back around, I walked the short distance between us and stood next to her desk.

"Come over to my place about six o'clock tonight and we can talk."

"Aren't you worried about what people might think?"

"I know what they think already, but it's my home and at least there, we won't have to go through the gawking." Claire reached over with her left hand touching my right shoulder. "Besides, I've missed you."

"I'm a pretty good cook," I said. "You want me to cook supper?"

"You can cook?" she said, almost shocked by the offer.

"Yeah, but don't look so surprised."

Claire's eyes sparkled and her smile was magical as she moved closer and put her arms around my waist.

"Better plan on cooking breakfast, too," she said, looking up at me. "Let's make sure your alibi is good and solid this time."

Couldn't hurt.

Chapter Twenty-five

Cox's Food Store was busy on a late Friday afternoon with people shopping for the weekend. The aisles were crowded as I selected items to cook Claire one of my specialties, Beef Stroganoff. It would be a masterpiece, or as the French say, "chef d'oeuvre." Julia Childs would say, "You don't have to cook fancy or complicated masterpieces – just good food from fresh ingredients."

So, with that thought in mind, I headed for the produce department where I picked out a small yellow onion, some fresh broccoli, a head of iceberg lettuce, a vine ripened tomato, a bunch of green onions, and a package of cello carrots. On the way through the breads, I grabbed a loaf of French bread and tossed it into the basket. Then I had a decision to make. *Rice or egg noodles.* Some prefer white rice with Stroganoff, while others favor egg noodles. *What would Claire like?* The more I thought about it the more she seemed to be a noodles girl.

"Pat Cassidy!" a female voice said from behind me.

It was Claire's mother, Maggie. She pushed her shopping cart up the aisle toward me. I began to blush.

"What are ya doin' in town?"

"Uh…well…hi, Maggie."

She peered down at the contents of my basket.

"You're the last person on earth I'd ever expect to see at the grocery store."

My face was hot and I felt red as a beet. *Dad's voice was ringing in my ears. Always tell the truth, honesty is the best policy. If you tell the truth you'll never have anything to be embarrassed about.* The glow began to fade.

"I went to see Claire," I said. "She invited me over tonight and I'm going to cook for us."

Maggie grinned and leaned closer nudging me with her right arm.

"Sooooo glad you're doing this, Pat."

"Thanks, Maggie, me too."

Maggie checked the aisle to see if anyone else was coming down B4.

"Claire really needs this," Maggie said with a soft voice.

"I understand, Maggie. Or, at least I do now."

"It's been hard for her, you know. You got to go off to Fort Worth and be the big hero. All people talk about around here is how you two were together while a triple murder was taking place."

"They better never say that around me or I'll punch their lights out."

"I know you would, darlin'. Just be careful with Claire. She likes you a whole a lot."

"I like her, too."

"We'll see, but y'all have a good time tonight. And, by the way," Maggie looked up at the shelf, "she likes egg noodles."

She must have been reading my mind. Uh-oh.

Maggie pushed her shopping cart past me and turned the corner.

Somewhat flustered, I pulled out the grocery list in my back pocket and checked it for good measure. Still on the list were powdered milk, beef broth, a can of Campbell's tomato soup, mushrooms, butter, sour cream, and a pound of sliced tenderloin. By the time I reached the meat counter I had everything I needed, except the meat. The butcher noticed I was searching for something and asked if he could help me find anything.

"Thanks," I said. "Yeah...I need about a pound of sliced tenderloin."

"How would you like it sliced?' he said amiably.

"An inch wide in two and half inch strips," I said.

"I'm Clint Bush."

"Pat Cassidy," I said, reaching across the meat counter to shake his hand.

"I thought that was you. J.T. and I are friends and I've seen you in the paper and on T.V. a time or two."

"Glad that's all over now...I'm ready to blend in with the furniture again."

"I'll bet that's right, but it was an interesting story to follow."

Clint was around thirty and combed his short brown hair neatly to the side. He was about six feet tall and he wore a white butcher jacket that was unsoiled. He walked to the back of the butcher shop and put an apron over his jacket and tied it around his waist. Clint stepped into a walk-in refrigerator and came back out with a loin of beef and placed it on the butcher block.

"Come on back and let's talk while I work," Clint said.

The meat counter had an open space at the end of it, so I made my way into the butcher block area and stood watching him slice the meat across the grain into long chunks.

"J.T. and I play on a semi-pro baseball team."

"Yeah…he's quite the athlete," I said.

"The team's made up of guys just like me," Clint said. "We have our day jobs, but still like to play a little baseball. You ever play any ball?"

"Little League, Pony League, played on my high school team."

"And…you were a boxer, too, I hear."

I gave him a bashful nod.

"A National Golden Gloves Heavyweight Champion J.T. tells me."

"Once upon a time," I said.

Clint took the long slices of beef and began to dice them into smaller cuts.

"I first heard J.T. was leaving us and going to work for you and Mr. Glasscock up in Fort Worth, but now I've heard he's stickin' around."

"When we talked earlier today he's still thinking it over."

"Are you going to be in town long?"

"I don't know…at least until I meet with Jeb tomorrow."

"We've got a game tomorrow night," Clint said. "Why don't you come and see us play?"

"You have a game tomorrow night?" I said.

Ahhhh…that's why J.T. didn't want to leave until Monday!

"We'll see," I said.

"After the game we all get together over at my place," Clint said, still slicing the tenderloin. "I always grill up some burgers and we sit around talking about the game and drink beer. You're invited if you want to come."

"Let me see what Jeb has on his mind tomorrow."

And what Claire has in store for me tonight.

Chapter Twenty-six

Claire's house was located a third of the way up the 2000 block of Walnut Street. I parked in her driveway and carried the bags in from the front seat of the Malibu. Thick Indian Hawthorns with pink blooms decorated the front of the white brick home and Dusty Millers lined the flower bed where, at the end of it, a rose bush flourished with delicate white petals. Large live oak trees provided ample shade in the front yard and on each side of the property line. Claire opened the front door as I stepped up onto the porch. She pointed me in the direction of the kitchen, where I toted the night's goodies and began removing everything from the paper bags.

"Wow," Claire said. "You really go all out."

"The only way I know how to do things."

"I know," she said, playfully. "What do you need?"

"That's a loaded question," I said.

"Let me rephrase the question. What do you need to cook dinner?"

"Show me where you keep your spices, pots and pans, and utensils."

"I have everything you need."

"I know you do."

"Aren't you the tiger tonight?"

"Something about cooking for a gorgeous woman brings out the bestial in me."

Claire grinned with coltish eyes and pointed out where everything in the kitchen was kept.

"How long till dinner?"

"About an hour or so," I said.

"See you in an hour."

"Where are you going?"

"I'm going to retire to my bedroom and get ready for the evening."

"It takes you that long?"

"Getting ready for you does."

Claire disappeared into the bedroom and the cooking began. The kitchen was roomy with a great view of her patio from the window above the sink. An old Zenith AM radio with an aqua chassis, white facing, and worn around the knobs, sat at the end of the kitchen counter. Billy Miller was chattering away on the radio when I turned it on.

"Rangers and Twins comin' up in about an hour here on KBRW as the Majors get underway tonight. It'll be Gaylord Perry pitching for the Rangers and Bert Blyleven on the mound for the Twins with Dick Risenhoover callin' the balls and strikes."

With the radio on in the background, I searched through the cabinets next to the stove and found an iron skillet where the pots and pans were kept and placed it on the stove top. I seasoned the meat and let it sit while I enjoyed a Coors that I picked up at the liquor store along with a bottle of burgundy wine. *That would be for later.* I placed a couple of sauce pans on top of the range and added butter to one, cooking oil to the other, and enough oil to cover the bottom of the iron skillet.

Billy came out of a commercial break and played a slow singing jingle. "*K...B...R...W...four...teen...nine...tee....*" The record he played was 'Till the Rivers All Run Dry' by Don Williams.

I turned the gas burners on under the sauce pans and skillet. Once the butter was melted and the oil was hot, I added flour to the sauce pans, and whipped them smooth with a wire whip to make a roux. When the skillet was hot, I began to braise the meat. The tenderloin cuts were sizzling in the skillet, when I realized I hadn't called Jeb to let him know I had made it into town.

When I picked up the receiver of the beige wall phone to call him, I heard a woman's voice say, "Is that Pat Cassidy over at your house?"

Claire was giggling as I quietly put the receiver back on its hook leaving them to their girl talk and went about dissolving milk powder in water and opening the beef broth. The milk powder mixture went into the butter roux and the beef broth into the cooking oil roux.

As I finished off the bottle of beer and gazed out Claire's

kitchen window, the shaded backyard was beginning to lose the light of day. In a few minutes the rouxes took on a gravy texture.

"Last week's number one song," Billy Miller said on the radio, "gives way to this week's number one from Freddie Fender. 'You'll Lose a Good Thing' on your Bicentennial Station KBRW."

After adding salt and white pepper to each roux, and sugar to the butter roux, I turned off the heat and set them aside. The meat continued to cook, so I opened another Coors and prepared the salad and fresh vegetables to cook. Then I sliced and buttered the French bread to bake.

In the dining room I set the table and lit the candles Claire had already placed in the center of the table. I opened the bottle of wine and dimmed the lights to low. It was a matter of adding all the ingredients to complete the Stroganoff. Drain the braised tenderloin; add the onions, white and brown sauce, tomato soup, mushrooms, and just the right amount of sour cream. The next step was to cook the egg noodles and fresh vegetables as the Stroganoff simmered over low heat. Dick Risenhoover was introducing the game broadcast from Arlington Stadium as I finished the meal preparation by chopping some green onion tops and parsley for garnishing the main course.

Claire came out of her bedroom with her hair up in a twist, wearing a powder blue velvet jump suit that zipped down the front and complemented her eyes. It fit well along the curves of her hour glass figure. Her makeup was perfect.

"You've been busy," she said.

"So have you, I see."

"Will you pour me a glass of wine?" she asked.

"I think that's possible."

The Coors in my hand was almost empty, so I finished it off and went to the dining room and poured us both a glass of wine. Claire took the loops holding the backdoor curtains off their hooks and let the separated curtains fall together to close out the world. Then she sat down at the table. I joined her as she sipped from the wine glass.

"What made you come see me?" Claire said, with big-eyed curiosity.

"J.T. said you asked about me."

"I did," Claire said. "I was wondering what you were up to after everything that happened out at Bobby's and up in Fort Worth was resolved."

"I spent a few days at my Dad's lake house trying to pull my head together."

"Did it help?"

"Some, but my head still isn't quite where it needs to be."

"I heard you were in town earlier this week," Claire said.

"Is that all it was?" I said, and took a sip of wine.

"What do you mean?"

"So much has happened this week that it seems like a long time ago now."

"J.T. mentioned you went on to Austin to look for Kerry Vogel."

"Let's not talk about that right now," I said. "Let's talk about you."

In the dim candlelight I noticed Claire's color subtly flame around the checks as she sipped the burgundy.

"Pat, I'm a big girl, but I never had any idea what it was like to be the center of the rumor mill."

"Do you think the rumoring will eventually go away?"

"Probably," Claire said, forcing a smile. "You being here right now makes it seem a lot better."

"Don't put too much stock into that, Claire."

She looked away from me as her forced smile turned to a frown, staring at her wine glass.

"Wow," she said, "you're direct aren't you?"

"I have to be at this point," I said. "I just don't know how much I have to give to a woman right now."

A smile returned to her face as she glanced over at me, and said, "You have quite a lot to give a girl."

I started to say 'Not in my present frame of mind' until I realized she was teasing with me.

Grinning back at her, I said, "Well, there is that."

"If that's all there can be between us right now," Claire said. "I'll take it."

The meal went off like a song, but neither of us ate very much. We talked about the things we had in common like our favorite music, books, and movies. With the meal complete, we rinsed the dishes and pots and pans. Claire lit a candle in the living room and dimmed the lights. She sat on the couch and watched me flip through her albums next to the stereo. I placed the Eagles' Greatest Hits record on the turntable and sat next to her. By the middle of side two, our arms were around each other and the kissing became more passionate. The music fed our excitement for each other.

All alone at the end of an evening...and the bright lights have faded to blue...I was thinking...'bout a woman...who might have loved me...and I never knew...

Claire pulled away from me breathing heavily and trying to catch her breath. She turned around and leaned her back against me. As I gently kissed the back of her neck, she slowly unzipped her top, and then fell back into my arms as we kissed intensely. A few minutes later I stood up with Claire in my arms and carried her to the bedroom.

Chapter Twenty-seven

Claire and I lay next to each other bound together by a tangled sheet. My breathing had almost returned to normal when she snuggled back up next to me and put her head on my left shoulder. A candle flickered on the dresser casting exotic shadows along the walls.

"Where did you learn to…cook like that?" Claire said under her breath, as she gasped for air.

I glanced at her face full of afterglow and kissed her forehead.

"There for a moment I thought you were going to ask me something else," I said.

She raised her head slightly and whispered into my ear, "Some things just come naturally."

Claire moved her head away from my shoulder and used her elbow to hold herself up. She had a puzzled look on her face as the sheet slipped off her shoulders and down to her thin waist.

"What?" I said.

"What's going on with your life right now?"

"What do you mean?"

"You seem different…I can't quite put my finger on it."

My better judgment kept me from turning that statement into something sexual.

"Someone a lot smarter than me once said, 'with a restless soul that follows rapacious dreams, we wander through life aimlessly,'" I quoted, instead.

Claire lay back down next to me placing her head on my shoulder.

"I think he also said, 'the walls we build around us to keep out the sadness also keep out the joy.'"

We didn't say anything for a long while.

"It's just lately," I said, "I've begun to feel changes in me I'm not so sure I like."

"Since Brett's murder."

"Yeah, I suppose that's when it started."

Claire was silent as she slowly rubbed her hand across my chest.

"I was one of those guys," I said, "who came home from Vietnam with his head screwed on the right way. I went over there, did my job, and came home secure in the belief that what I did was the honorable thing."

"What has changed?"

"I'm not sure. Maybe it has something to with the kind of man I became during my tour of duty."

Claire's circular motion on my chest became slow tight spirals with her fingertips.

"That man is not the Pat Cassidy you know today," I said. "I left that man behind and never looked back, but lately the man I see in the mirror is beginning to resemble him again. I just can't believe how easy it is for me to kill a man and not feel any remorse."

I could feel Claire's body ever so slightly flinch with the comment. She settled back on her pillow pulling the sheet up to her neck as my share of the cotton linen went with her.

"Pat, it's difficult for me to listen to you talk about this stuff."

"Maybe I shouldn't talk to you about it then," I said.

Claire sat up and propped her back against a pillow and the headboard.

"No, I want you talk about it," she said, determined to hear me out.

"I feel even more hardened and bitter since Calloway and Big Jake were brought to justice. I really believed my life would return to the way it was before everything happened."

"But it hasn't," Claire said.

"Uh-uh," I said, shaking my head.

"Pat," she said, touching my shoulder with her right hand, "it's obvious you are troubled about a lot of things. Maybe you need some professional help."

I sat up in the bed and stared at her. "Are you saying I need a shrink?"

"Maybe," Claire said. "Listen, and God knows, I'm not all together either, but you are a paradox, Mr. Cassidy."

"Explain to me what you mean," I said.

"You are one of the sweetest men I've ever known," Claire said, "but…"

"But what?"

"It's so obvious how devastated you are about Brett's death, but yet you say you can kill another man without feeling any remorse. How can you have so much compassion for one man and none for the other?"

"Well, I guess you've got me pretty well figured out."

"No, I don't have you figured out," Claire said. "I just know that when you make love to me you are tender…and gentle…and loving."

"You know, Claire," I said, "there's something about the way you called me 'Mr. Cassidy' that really turns me on."

Claire moved smoothly toward me and settled into my arms until we were face to face. I looked at the shadow around her eyes in the faint candlelight and kissed her. Then we made love again.

Chapter Twenty-eight

Saturday morning I left Claire's house to meet Jeb downtown. He was sitting in his new burnt orange 1976 Ford F250 Camper Special with a CB radio wire whip antenna sticking up from the middle of the white roof. I parked across the street and walked over and stood by the driver's side window. Jeb stuck out his left hand and patted me on the arm as he held the CB microphone in his right hand.

"Good to see you, Pat, be right with you. Come back on that," Jeb said, clicking the mic.

A male voice blurted through the speaker in response to his 'Come back on that.'

"It sounds like you need some hamburger helper, Good Buddy."

That meant Jeb's signal was a little weak.

"Saw some Schneider Eggs on the way in this mornin' may wanna slow it down on the way in," Jeb transmitted.

Jeb was telling him there was a construction site on the way into town with orange barrels filled with sand and men at work.

"10-4, Good Buddy," Jeb's CB friend said.

Jeb looked up at me and made a funny expression.

"Animal, you might wanna stop for some mud until it clears."

Jeb was telling 'Animal' he should stop for a cup a coffee until the traffic was moving a little faster.

"Will do, Tycoon, see you on the flip-flop."

"This is frequency twenty-seven point two-fifteen channel thirty-one signing off," Jeb said, ending the conversation with Animal.

Jeb hung up the microphone on a magnetic clip mounted on the front of the dashboard.

"Come with me, Pat," he said, getting out of his truck.

Jeb was dressed the part of a hard working rancher with his scuffed up brown cowboy boots, worn long sleeve denim shirt, and faded jeans. He put on his straw Stetson as he got out of his truck. We walked to the end of the block and onto the driveway of a dilapidated service station that had been boarded up for years. The front of the building was cattycornered with the canopy and the driveway equally accessible from both streets. Two ancient red faded gas pumps sitting near the outer edge of the canopy stood as if they were on an eternal vigil.

"This was my father's service station," Jeb said with a melancholy look on his face.

The front windows were shuttered and the glass in the front door and double bay garage doors was clouded with age.

"My very first job was here pumpin' gas for my Pappy back during the depression."

I nodded.

"He wasn't just a service station owner you know. Pappy was the Mobil Oil consignee for Brownwood and sold tires and auto parts."

Jeb pointed at the old gas pumps, "Back then it was Mobilgas. See those old signs at the top of the pumps?"

The Mobilgas logo sat inside a white circular sign with the familiar image of Pegasus, the winged horse from Greek mythology. Supposedly, Pegasus was sired by Poseidon, the horse-god. There would be an inspiring spring burst forth wherever the winged horse struck its hoof.

"He probably did well for himself then," I said.

"He did, Pat. Everything I am is because of him."

"It sounds like he was a really great man."

"Pappy said he pumped gas into the first automobile in Brownwood."

I nodded again, this time with a smile.

"This was his first service station and his best one, but he owned several all over Brown County," Jeb continued. "I've been holdin' on to this place for sentimental reasons for nearly twenty years."

"Are you going to sell it?"

"Hell, no, Pat. But I've gotta make a decision to do something with it."

"Why, what's going on?"

"This whole block from here to the end of the next block is gonna be renovated. Me and a couple of investors are fixin' it all up to make it better. So, Pappy's old station has to go or I'll need to remodel it and make it look nice."

"Is this where you want me to set up my office?"

"I want to show you something, Pat."

Jeb reached in his pocket and pulled out his keys and unlocked the front door. Dust fell off the top of the door as he reached into the semi-darkness of the boarded up office to find the light switch. The office was completely empty. A wall separated the office area from the garage. Double swinging doors with round windows led into the double bay garage. The bay area was also empty except for a drive up ramp that predated the pressure lifts you see in service stations today.

"It's old, I know," Jeb said, "but I've kept it clean through the years except for a little dust."

He turned and walked back into the office and turned right down a dark hallway. By the time I followed him into the office, he had turned on the hallway light.

"Over here, Pat. Watch your step goin' up these steps. They're pretty steep."

At the top of the stairs I stepped up into a large open warehouse with tall wide windows.

"This is where Pappy stored his tires and auto parts."

"What do you have in mind, Jeb?"

"There's plenty of room up here to build ya a nice apartment and office."

"What about downstairs?"

"Here's the part I think you're really gonna like. I know how much you and J.T. like to work out and throw a little leather at each other once in awhile."

I nodded in agreement.

"I'll build a gym in the old office and put a boxing ring in the garage. Maybe you and J.T. can start a boxin' team in your spare time to work with our young boys."

"You'd do all this for us?"

"When I'm through with this place you won't recognize it. It'll be classy and homey. So…how 'bout it? Whaddya think?"

"I don't know, Jeb. It all sounds like a wonderful idea, but I'm not sure about living in Brownwood."

"Think about it, Pat. After you're finished lookin' for Sheriff Vogel's son, let's sit down and talk about it again. By the way, how's that goin'?"

I hit the high points and brought him up-to-date including the part about covering Buddy Connors' hospital bill.

"You are comin' out to the ranch for supper tonight, aren't ya?" Jeb said.

"Thanks, but I have plans to watch J.T. play baseball tonight."

"Well…you wanna spend the night at the ranch, or are you stayin' with J.T.?"

"Not exactly," I said, trying to avoid telling him anything else.

"Ohhhhh…never mind, son," Jeb said, smiling. "Hell, I used to be young once."

Chapter Twenty-nine

The spring day had turned into an Indian summer and on Jeb's Brownwood radio station, newsman Val Debose was delivering the noon news.

"Clear skies and unseasonably warm with the high today in the upper 80s and the low tonight in the mid-50s. Wind will be light and variable. Currently the wind is calm and the temperature is already at seventy-nine degrees. That's the latest look at news and weather from your Bicentennial Station...KBRW. Stay tuned...Lone Star Radio Network news is next."

I had heard on the radio earlier in the morning the Rangers won their season opener last night, two to one, over the Twins. Listening to baseball was not a part of last night's planned activities, but the season was underway and the fresh smell of spring had tantalized my senses, putting me in the mood to go to a game. So I decided to accept Clint Bush's invitation to watch him and J.T. play some ball.

Claire was in her front yard planting flowers when I pulled up into her driveway. I just sat in the car admiring the view when she stood up and made her way over to me. Claire was stunning, wearing a dark blue spaghetti strap halter top and white short shorts. Fashionable sunglasses accented her lovely face and her hair was again up in a twist. I got out of the car and leaned against the door.

"You could stop traffic in that outfit," I said.

"I've been known to," Claire teased.

"I can believe it."

"Mama always said a woman's beauty doesn't last forever."

"You'll always be a beautiful woman, Claire."

"I'm twenty-six, Pat. Tell me that in thirty years."

"Don't rush things."

"Take off your sunglasses," Claire said.

I took off my sunglasses and put them in my shirt pocket.

"I've never seen your eyes in broad daylight."

"The eyes are the window of the soul," I said.

"You have the most penetrating green eyes I've ever seen."

I halfway grinned.

"Your hair in this light," Claire said, "is almost blonde. I always thought your hair was brown."

"Are you flirting with me?" I said.

"Oh, yes…in the light of day you're even better looking than I thought."

"You're embarrassing me," I said, feeling flushed in the face. "Do you have any plans for tonight?"

"Just to be with you if you're going to be around."

"You want to go to a baseball game?"

"You want to take me to a baseball game?" Claire said, laughing.

"I just thought we should go out," I said. "We can't stay hidden away in your bedroom forever."

"There are worse things," Claire said.

"You're right about that."

"What time is the game?"

"Seven o'clock," I said.

"Well, then…that gives us the rest of the afternoon to find something to do. You know the third time is a charm."

I think she's lost count.

Chapter Thirty

Claire and I sat in the bleachers watching people come into the ballpark. The smell of popcorn filled the air and the lights were on as the warm day slipped into evening. Under the lights, the team from San Angelo was taking infield when J.T. and Clint walked up to the chain-link fence backstop.

"Hey, Cassidy," J.T. said. "You interested in playing some ball tonight?"

J.T. glanced at Clint standing next to him, a little uncomfortable with the request.

Clint said, "We've only got eight players. We'll have to forfeit if we don't come up with another player."

"You've got to be kidding," I said.

"I wish I was," Clint said.

Claire nudged me, "Go on...it'll be fun."

"What about you?"

"I'll be fine. When Clint's wife gets here I'll sit with her."

"What about a uniform and glove?" I said.

"I've got a uniform in my trunk," Clint said.

"Yeah...and we'll come up with a glove," J.T. added.

"What about cleats?"

"What's your shoe size?" Clint said.

"Size thirteen."

"Got an extra pair but they'll be too small for you."

"You've got on black tennis shoes. You'll be fine, Cassidy," J.T. said.

"Sure, why not? I could use the exercise."

Clint gave me a gold cap, pullover jersey, and leggings, as well as a white pair of baseball pants. I suited out in the restroom and joined the team in the dugout. J.T. handed me a first baseman's mitt.

"I'm playing first base?"

"No," Clint said, "you're playing left field."

"I'm playing left field with a first baseman's mitt?"

"That's the only extra glove we have," J.T. said.

"O.K., guys, let's hit the field," Clint said.

We fell behind one to nothing in the top of the first inning. J.T. singled in the bottom half of the inning, but was left on base. Clint had me batting fifth in the line up so I came to bat in the top of the second. The opposing pitcher was short and stocky and threw a lot of curve balls.

"He likes to throw the curve, Pat," Clint said, as I grabbed a thirty-six inch bat and walked toward the batter's box.

A fast ball greeted me on the first pitch for a called strike. The second pitch was another fast ball which I felt good about fouling off down the right field line. The third pitch was a curve ball which I swung at, missing badly, for strike three.

The San Angelo team was threatening again in the top of the third with runners at first and second base and one out, when the batter fouled a pitch down the left field side that was curving out of play. I sprinted to the fence and reached over as far as I could and made a snow cone catch for the out, thanks to the long webbing of the mitt. Russell, our third baseman, drifted over and saw the catch from only a few feet away.

"He got it!" Russell shouted. "He caught it! Two outs."

The next batter hit a ground ball in Clint's direction at shortstop. Sliding to his left, he fielded the grounder and threw out the runner and the inning was over. Clint and I got a few slaps on the back in the dugout for our defensive plays.

Leading off the fifth inning and still down by one, I watched the first two pitches miss on the outside corner of the plate. Figuring the pitcher didn't want to fall behind three and oh in the count, I anticipated a fast ball across the plate. The pitch hung up in the strike zone and I swung at it as hard as I could, ripping a long drive to left-center field that bounced once and hopped over the fence for a ground rule double. Clint stepped up and laced a double down the right field line and I easily scored from second base. Russell followed in the lineup and delivered a single to right-centerfield that scored Clint and we had a two to one lead.

Holding on to a one run lead in the top of the eighth inning, San Angelo threatened loading the bases with two outs. Clint, from his shortstop position, waved me in to play shallow. On a two-one count, the batter hit a blooper just past Russell at third base. Charging in from left field I dove, extending as far as I could, and the ball dropped into my mitt. I hit the ground and rolled over on my back, holding the ball inside my glove in the air. Russell helped me up off the ground, and he, along with Clint and J.T., celebrated the catch as we jogged to the dugout. Claire and the rest of the home crowd were on their feet and I pointed at her with big smile on my face.

Clint called the team together in the dugout and told us we had a problem.

"Gene's arm is gone," he said. "Can anyone pitch?"

"I can't," J.T. said. "That's why I play second base. My arm can't reach much past first."

"I can't pitch either," Clint said.

Everyone shook their head.

"I can pitch," I said.

"You ever pitched before?" Clint asked.

"Yeah…I used to pitch for my Pony League team. But that was a long time ago."

"Go warm up," Clint said, handing me a baseball.

My first pitch in the top of the ninth inning was a knuckle ball that the batter watched float over the plate for a called strike. The second pitch was a fast ball that he fouled off against the backstop. I threw him another knuckle ball on the third pitch and he popped it up to Clint.

One down, two to go.

The next batter went after my curve ball on the first pitch and grounded out to J.T. at second base, and just like that, we had two outs. That brought up the guy who had gone three for three for San Angelo. As he stood in, I thought about what I should throw him. He seemed to be able to hit anything, so I decided to throw him a fast ball, which he swung on and fouled off out of play. Throwing him another fast ball, he fouled it off. *Strike two.* Surprisingly, I had him off balance. I went back to the knuckle ball and as I released the pitch it felt like it was going to be high in the strike zone. The batter hesitated, and then took a rip at it, missing it badly for strike three. I kicked the ground with a skip in celebration and felt like a kid again.

Later in the evening the guys lounged around the patio watching Clint grill burgers, drinking beer, and talking about the game. Claire and the other girlfriends and wives were in the house preparing everything else that would go with the meal.

"You can play for us anytime," Clint said, flipping burgers.

I nodded thinking about the possibility while I enjoyed a Lone Star Longneck.

"Is there anything you can't do?" J.T. said.

"Yes. I can't leap tall buildings with a single bound."

The guys standing near the grill laughed.

"No, really, it was nothing," I said. "It was just my night. You guys have a great team."

"Maybe you should consider moving to Brownwood," Clint said, "instead of J.T. moving to Fort Worth."

I tried to imagine what that would be like considering Jeb's offer earlier in the day.

"How are you and Claire getting along now?" J.T. said.

"We're O.K.,' I said.

"It looks like more than O.K.," Clint chimed in. "Don't take this the wrong way, but Claire is vah-vah-ka-boom…if you know what I mean."

Russell's bravado laugh overpowered the other laughs and chuckles that came from the guys who found Clint's playful comment funny.

"No…shit," Russell said.

I just smiled thinking about the way Claire and I spent the afternoon.

"J.T. tells me you're trying to find Kerry Vogel," Clint said.

"We both are…that is…as of Monday."

"Most of the guys here went to high school with Kerry and some of us played ball with him. Gene over there played baseball with him."

"I played football *and* baseball with him," Russell said.

"Kerry, J.T, and I were all four sport lettermen," Clint said.

Out of Touch

"I picked up his trail last week in Austin when I was...," I paused and looked around at the guys and made a funny face, "while I was *investigatin'*."

There were a few laughs and chuckles.

"That a fact?" Russell said. "Do you know what happened to him?"

"I think I do, but I'm not quite sure. Time will only tell."

"Time is his biggest enemy," Clint said, as he hung his spatula on the side of the grill. "Don't you figure Kerry is dead after all this time?"

"We don't know, Clint," J.T. interjected between sips of beer. "Pat has gotten the attention of someone who wants to see *him* dead."

"Geezzzz, Cassidy," Russell said. "I've never known a man so many people want to see dead."

Male or female?

Chapter Thirty-one

Claire sat on the living room couch with her bare legs tucked underneath her, wearing an amethyst Babydoll nightie that tied at the bust. It had proven to be irresistible after we returned from the Bush's last night. I fixed us a brunch of scrambled eggs, bacon, toast, coffee, and orange juice and placed it on the coffee table.

"I have to go back to Fort Worth today."

"When will you be back?" Claire said, touching my hair at the back of the collar.

I drank some coffee.

"I don't know, Claire."

"Will you ever come back?"

"Of course," I said, "if anything else, I'll want to see you again."

Claire leaned toward me and we kissed.

"I've got a decision to make," I said.

"I hope you decide to move to Brownwood," Claire said.

"I know you do," I said. "I'm beginning to see that living here wouldn't be so bad after all."

I ate some of my scrambled eggs and toast.

"My home is in Forth Worth though," I said. "I was born there…grew up there…all my friends are there."

Claire gave me a '*what about your friends here*' look.

"Well, except for my friends here," I said.

"Your friends are not exclusively in Fort Worth," Claire said. "You have friends you've made in broadcasting…friends you made in the Army…fighting in the Golden Gloves…and your other travels."

I drank the small glass of orange juice sitting on the coffee table.

"Just because you've lived most of your life in Fort Worth up to this point, doesn't mean that's where you should make your home for the rest of your life."

"I have to go back to Fort Worth and talk to my Dad," I said. "I've asked him to come in on this endeavor with me, but I can tell you for a fact, he will never leave Forth Worth."

Claire picked up a piece of toast taking a small bite.

"But his life isn't yours."

I finished off my coffee.

"I belong in Fort Worth," I said, looking at Claire. "I already had things rolling there before I left and went to Austin last week. Wynn thinks we're setting up our office in Fort Worth."

"So, you've pretty well made your mind up," Claire said.

"Yes," I said.

Claire and I finished breakfast and got ready for the day ahead of us. A little before eleven in the morning I had my suitcase packed and was dressed in my blue blazer, white dress shirt, khakis, brown boots, with the nine millimeter holstered underneath my left arm. Claire had changed into a pair of jeans and a cute maroon t-shirt with the script 'Western Heights Elementary Teachers are Cool.' I held her in my arms and kissed her for a long time. Then I just held her close.

"Do you have to carry that thing?" Claire said, laughing. "It's poking me."

I laughed with her.

"Yes…it has saved my life more than once."

"Let's just hope you never have to use it again."

"Let's," I said.

Chapter Thirty-two

By mid-afternoon I was back in Fort Worth so I stopped at Ernie's Bar and Grill for a beer. A few of the regulars sitting at the bar greeted me when I sat down. The Sunday afternoon crowd watched the Rangers and Twins on the television sets above the bar. Toby Harrah for the Rangers was up to bat in the bottom of the eighth inning with the score tied at three.

"It's been real quiet here since you ain't been around stirrin' up somethin'," said Mammoth Mike, Ernie's bartender.

"Well, we'll see what I can stir up before the night is up."

"Just let me know so I can get out of the way. What's your pleasure today, Pat?"

"Heineken on tap and I need to use your phone."

Mike drew a tall glass of Heineken and set it on a small napkin. I took a drink of the beer and Mike placed a black phone within reach on the bar. I punched line one and called Dad at home. There was no answer so I called him at the lake house.

"Hello," a woman's voice said answering the phone.

"Mrs. Branch," I said. "You picked up on the wrong ring again."

"Is this, Pat?" Mrs. Branch said.

"Yes, it is."

"It is so good to hear your voice again," Mrs. Branch said.

"Thank you," I said. "Now will you hang up so I can call Dad back?"

"I'm sorry," Mrs. Branch said. "I'm hard of hearing these days and don't distinguish the party line rings as well as I used to."

"Hello," Dad said.

"You can hang up now, Mrs. Branch," I said. "Dad's on the line. Nice talking to you."

"Well...O.K.," she said.

Dad and I listened until we heard her receiver hang up.

"Hi, son, how was Austin?"

"Austin was very interesting, but I spent the weekend in Brownwood."

"We need to talk," Dad said.

"When will you be back from the lake?"

"Tomorrow morning, say around ten."

"I'll see you at the house," I said.

After I hung up, Mike moved the phone off the bar and placed it on the counter behind him, pushing the phone cord out of the way with his foot.

"What's Pat Cassidy been up to lately?" Mike asked.

"A little of this...a little of that...and a whole bunch of no good."

"Sounds like the Pat I know," Mike said.

"Is Ernie coming in today?"

"He called an hour or so ago and said he'd been in to do the week's inventory about three-thirty."

The familiar Pearl Beer clock above the mirror behind the bar told me Ernie would be here in just a few minutes. In the meantime I drank beer and thought about Claire. On the TV, the Twins scored a run in the top of the ninth inning and took a four to three lead over the Rangers. Ernie came into the bar through the kitchen door and smiled when he saw me.

"So the prodigal son returns," Ernie said.

"I was that bad of a son?" I said.

"Whatever that means," Ernie said.

"It means…," I looked at Ernie and decided not to pursue it and shook it off with a waving motion.

Ernie appeared a little puzzled.

"The rumor mill has been spinning about Emmett."

"There are rumors going around about Dad?"

"Oh, no," Ernie said, "I didn't mean it like that. The word is getting around that the mayor is going to appoint your dad to be Chief of Police of the Fort Worth Police Department."

"Mayor Castleberry is going to make my dad the Chief?"

"That's what I hear," Ernie said. "Says he wants to clean up the police department and the best man for the job is your dad."

"I'm surprised he hasn't said anything to me about it."

"You've been out of town, haven't you?"

"Yeah, I was in Austin for most of last week, and then went on to Brownwood for the weekend."

"Sounds like you and your dad need to talk more often," Ernie said, eyeing each person sitting at the bar.

"I just talked to him."

"He say anything to you about it?"

"Just that he needed to talk to me," I said.

"Well, there you go. Where's he at?"

"The lake house, fishing."

"When's he comin' back?"

"Dad said he would be back in the morning."

"It's best to get it straight from the horse's mouth anyway. If there is anything to the rumor then he can set the record straight."

"Dad is good at that."

"*That's* the reason Mayor Castleberry wants him to be his chief."

Chapter Thirty-three

Emmett Cassidy joined the Fort Worth Police Department after completing the police academy and graduating first in his class. He became a detective shortly before the Kennedy assassination and was on special detail the day the president landed in Fort Worth to begin his fateful trip to Dallas. He became Inspector Emmett Cassidy, head of robbery and homicide, while I was in Vietnam. After less than four months of retirement, he was now being called back to the department to serve as its chief.

It was a little after eleven in the morning and we were having lunch at Alma's, a restaurant frequented by policemen, firemen, and other city workers because of its location near city hall. Dad was drinking coffee with cream and two sugars. I drink my coffee black.

"Castleberry called me Saturday morning," Dad said, scanning the dining room for familiar faces.

His face was tanned from a week of fishing at the lake and his brown hair was neat and parted to the side. Touches of gray highlighted his sideburns. Just inside the restaurant front door, his brown Fedora with white pinstripes hung on a hat rack. It went well with the camel shade sport coat and bistre colored slacks he was wearing. The ecru dress shirt was open at the collar, crisply starched, and Dad had on a new pair of Bass Tassel Loafers. Obviously, he had been shopping for new clothes. *But he'll have to get used to wearing a tie again.*

"You talked about it over the phone?" I said.

"No…that wouldn't be wise since the lake phone is on a party line. He drove all the way to the lake to talk to me 'mano a mano.'"

"Are you going to take the job?"

"I am," Dad said. "The city has had a crooked mayor running it far too long and Castleberry is determined to clean up city hall. He said he wants me to do the same thing with the police department."

Alma, the owner, was behind the counter talking with three fireman enjoying lunch. We made eye contact and she waved with a hospitable smile. I acknowledged her neighborly gesture with a wave that resembled more of a salute.

"I am happy for you, Dad. You deserved that job a long time ago, but I was counting on your expertise to do this new job for Jeb."

"I realize that, but you know as well I do…this is the job I'm supposed to be doing."

Dad's blue eyes inspected my expression searching for some kind of inclination of how I was taking the news. After all, he's very good at reading people.

"J.T. is having second thoughts as well," I said. "He's going to help me find Kerry, but after that he wasn't sure."

"So you're worried about doing the job Jeb has handed you without us?"

"Yes," I said.

He finished his coffee and set the cup back down, sliding the cup and saucer to the edge of the table so the waitress would see he needed a refill. She came over and filled his cup and gave him a couple of fresh creamers. The waitress pointed the coffee pot at me and asked if I wanted a refill. I shook my head.

"When you came home from Vietnam, what did I tell you?" Dad said.

"You told me I should think about becoming a cop."

"You wanted to pursue a radio career and I was all for it…except I believed you were meant to be…"

"A cop," I said, finishing his sentence.

"You're a natural, kiddo," Dad said. "You have the ability to sense things when no one else can, and you're the best shot I've ever seen. You don't need me, or J.T., to do this job. Just rely on your instinct."

"I was really looking forward to working with you."

"Thanks, but we'll have our opportunities to work together. What's going on with the Kerry Vogel case, anyway?"

"I think I have a lead."

"Like father, like son," Dad said. "Tell me about it."

"A religious cult, known as the Church of the Chosen, and a woman who goes by the name of Sister Charlene are somehow tied to Kerry's disappearance."

"I have heard of the 'Chosen' but the woman's name doesn't sound familiar."

"What do you know about them?" I said.

"Houston based, I believe," Dad said. "You can probably find out more about them down there."

"Yeah, I've already thought about that. I sent J.T. to Houston this morning."

"They swindled money from some rich folks a few years back and disappeared what seemed like overnight. We never could pin anything on them, much less find them."

"Ever heard of the 'Chosen's' leader, Reverend Malachi Jackson?"

"Yeah, I've heard of him, but that's about all," Dad said. "What's the connection with the Vogel kid?"

"A few days before he disappeared, this 'Sister Charlene' was seen handing out flyers at Memorial Stadium about the 'Chosen's' revival. I've also been told she had the body of a goddess."

Dad raised his eyebrows.

"Did the boy attend the revival?" Dad asked.

"No evidence to the contrary, but it's a plausible scenario. What I do know, is over the next few days, or there about, Kerry was heard talking to someone named Charlie on the pay phone in his dorm."

"Police back then find out who Charlie was?"

"No, it was a dead end."

The waitress asked if we were ready to order and Dad told her we were eating the buffet today.

"How did you find Sister Charlene?"

"Microfilm at the UT Library in a 1968 copy of the Austin American-Statesman."

"How many editions of the paper did you go through?"

"All of June and July of that year and part of August. I ran across a small advertisement in the classified section of the August eighth edition, and when I saw the name Sister Charlene, a bell went off."

"Good work," Dad said.

I told Dad everything else that happened surrounding the investigation in Austin.

"So your hunch is this religious cult is somehow involved in smuggling drugs into the United States and this boy…who is now a man…is somehow caught up in it."

"Something like that," I said.

"And…," Dad paused and ran the scenario around in his head, "this boy…who is now a grown man…is involved now because back in '68 this 'Sister Charlene' lured him to the revival and through religion and sex brainwashed him into becoming a follower of the church."

"Does it sound too farfetched?" I said.

"It would, except that something like that happened to Patty Hearst, and now she's in jail. Pat, if this boy is still alive, he is now as much a part of the 'Chosen' as this Sister Charlene, and the hold they have on him will not be easily broken. He will not want to come back to the life he once knew."

"Kerry's family doesn't have any money, Dad. Patty was held for ransom because the Symbionese Liberation Army knew her family could pay."

"Pat," he said, "a man's worth isn't always measured by the almighty dollar."

Chapter Thirty-four

My old space in the underground parking garage of the Glasscock Communication Center was empty and the Malibu almost parked itself. I took the elevator from the parking garage to the fourth floor where Dottie, the WFTW receptionist, greeted me when I walked through the front door.

"Glad to see you, Pat," Dottie said, smiling.

She was very good at that part of her job.

"Good to see you, too. Is Wynn around?"

"Yes, I'll buzz him and let him know you are here. He said he wanted to talk to you as soon as you arrived."

Dottie pushed the last button at the bottom of her phone and dialed Wynn's intercom number.

"Pat's here," she said to Wynn.

She listened for a moment and then sent me into his office. Wynn stood and greeted me with a smile and a handshake. He had on a pair of blue slacks with pinstripes and a stylish white long sleeve dress shirt with a button down collar. A light blue tie was loosened at the neck and a blue suit jacket that matched his slacks hung on a hanger behind his desk. Wynn's thick brown hair was combed nicely with a touch of Brylcreem and he was letting his sideburns grow longer.

"How have you been, Pat?"

"I'm fine, Wynn. What's on your mind?"

"Well, I guess you know you're a hot commodity right now and the station could use you back on the air."

"I don't think so," I said. "For the foreseeable future I'm going to concentrate on finding Kerry Vogel."

"I thought you would be biting at the bullet to get back on the air with us," Wynn said, settling back in his chair with a surprised look on his face.

"I have this case I'm working on and it's occupying almost all my time. Besides, Wynn, it was just last month that you sent me on my way down to Brownwood."

"Pat, you know we didn't have any other choice in the matter."

"Well, let me put it this way, Wynn, working for Jeb and living in Brownwood is starting to look better and better all the time."

"When we sent you off there last month you didn't feel that way."

"Things change."

Wynn leaned forward in his chair and pulled a sliding panel out of the right side of his desk, propped his feet up on it, and settled back into his chair again.

"What's changed?" he asked.

"Jeb has offered to build me an office and an apartment at a place there in the downtown area."

"Well, if Jeb is going to build it I know it will be nice and I know how much he would like to have you down there with him."

I nodded.

"But this is your home, Pat."

I nodded again.

"I understand that you're real busy with the job you have at hand in trying to find Sheriff Vogel's son, but this is going to be a great year for the Cowboys and I want to put you at the forefront of our coverage."

Wynn's background was in radio sales and I was getting the sales pitch.

"Talk to me," I said.

"They were just a few points away from winning it all last year and now they've got the number one draft choice."

"I know."

"Of course you do, Pat. I didn't mean to insinuate you didn't."

"Dallas will probably draft the kid from Pittsburgh that won the Heisman Trophy. That'll put them over the top next year."

"I want to put you on the air in afternoon drive time to talk sports."

"You mean you want me to do my own sports talk show?"

"Exactly," Wynn said, "use your knowledge of sports and talk live with the coaches, players, and fans. The ratings should go through the roof, especially with your name recognition right now."

"Wynn, I'm impressed. This is a really great idea and it sounds right up my alley."

"Will you do it, then?"

"When would you want to kick it off?"

"It's too late to help us with the spring ratings, so we're shooting for the first of July. That will get us established for the fall ratings period."

"I'm not committing to anything right now, Wynn."

"Take your time. July is a long way away."

I stood up and thanked him for thinking about me. Wynn walked around his desk and we shook hands.

"Keep me in touch on how things are going with your investigation and be sure and take a peek at what we've done to your office down the hall. We put down new carpet and slapped a couple of coats of paint on the walls. It looks great."

"Thanks, Wynn, appreciate it very much. The sports talk show idea is a stroke of genius."

"Thanks, but for the show to really be successful, it needs you."

"I'll let you know in a few weeks."

"All I ask is you think about it. You would be a natural."

I've heard that before.

Wynn opened the door to his office and I walked out and sat down on a chair in front of Dottie's desk.

"You said something the other day about a bunch of mail."

Dottie took off her glasses and turned away from her typewriter.

"How is Pat?" she said, playfully.

"Wondering why I ever let Jeb talk me into this new gig."

"Jeb is awfully persuasive."

"Tell me about it," I said.

"Here's your fan mail." She reached down and lifted a mail bag off the floor and dropped it on top of her desk. "This is for you and so is this stack of messages. Six, by the way, are from Paula Conn."

Chapter Thirty-five

Paula Conn was a reporter for Channel 8 in Dallas when I first met her. She vaulted to network television stardom with her coverage of the political scandal involving billionaire gubernatorial candidate Tom Calloway, the mayor of Fort Worth, and the Lone Star State's favorite son. He was rich, powerful, handsome, and a stone cold lead pipe lock to become the next governor of Texas. Calloway, along with a crooked union boss by the name of Big Jake Riley, conspired to steal the election and had my best friend murdered along the way. Paula, Dad, J.T. and I exposed both of them for what they were. Calloway is now facing multiple murder and racketeering charges and Riley is dead. Paula wanted to talk to me, but I didn't know why. I called the phone number she left in the messages but she wasn't available, so I left her a message. She would call me back.

Dad aimed his Smith and Wesson snub nose .38 at the target in the indoor firing range of the Fort Worth Shooting Club. We both wore protective glasses and ear plugs. Dad's Fedora was slightly pushed up. He always said he couldn't hit the broadside of a barn without his hat on. After emptying his revolver into the target, he put his gun down and removed his protective gear.

"I placed all six rounds in the bullseye," he said, reloading the .38.

Dad pushed a button and the target tracked toward us on a pulley that stopped in front of us.

"Nice shooting," I said.

"Fort Worth's top cop needs to be able to shoot," he said. "Now it's your turn."

Dad put his protective glasses back on and slipped in the earplugs. Pointing the nine millimeter, I zoned in on the bullseye, unloading the clip of thirteen rounds. When the last round discharged the slide locked back in a reloading position. We watched as the target scooted along a cable, stopped abruptly, and dangled on its clamp. The center of the bullseye had a circular pattern in the middle of it. Each shot had hit dead center.

"Remind me to never get into a pissing contest with you," Dad said.

"I will," I said, removing the earplugs.

"Have you checked on your blind informant since you left Austin?"

"Domingo Perez is making sure he is protected around the clock. We've talked every morning since I left Austin."

Dad took off his protective glasses.

"Perez sounds like a good cop," Dad said.

"He's a good man," I said.

"The Mexicans trying to wire your car with a bomb beat up the blind man, and then came back to the hospital to supposedly finish him off?"

"The best we can tell."

"Given that much thought?" Dad said.

"We did."

I pushed the release on the Browning and the slide popped back into place. Picking up a loaded clip, I reloaded and cocked a round into the chamber.

"Who are *we*?"

"Perez, his former partner at the Austin P.D, Detective Jack McKay, and me."

"Why didn't they finish off the blind man to begin with?"

I removed my protective glasses.

"Dad, the blind man's name is Buddy Connor."

"O.K.," he said, "Why didn't they finish off Buddy to begin with?"

"The best we could come up with was they were trying to draw me out."

"So, they beat him up because he'd been talking to you about the 'Chosen' and they figured sooner or later you'd come to his aid."

Dad clipped on fresh targets and we sent them both sliding back into ready position.

"Yes," I said, putting my glasses back on.

"How did these men know you had been asking questions about them?"

"Buddy said he was going to ask around about the 'Chosen' to see what he could find out for me."

"In doing so, he talked to someone that tipped them off," Dad surmised.

I nodded.

"But you didn't show up right away because you went to San Antonio and they probably thought if they went ahead and killed Buddy you would be certain to surface."

"Correct," I said.

"They show up at the hospital, but the nurse scared them away," Dad continued.

"She was very scary."

Dad smiled.

"You finally show up…and as the evening grew later, the parking lot empties, and they see it as a great opportunity to wire your car with a bomb."

"I believe that's the way it went down."

Dad put his protective glasses back on.

"Let's shoot," he said.

"The loser buys supper," I said.

"Well, I'm glad I have plenty of cash then."

Chapter Thirty-six

The next morning Dad left the house early for meetings with Mayor Castleberry. I fixed a breakfast of two eggs sunny side up, bacon, toast, orange juice, and coffee and sat at the kitchen table watching David Hartman interview decathlete Bruce Jenner. I thought about Hartman's TV drama 'Lucas Tanner' that was cancelled after one season just last year. *That was a really good show.* Jenner was the odds-on-favorite to win the Olympic Decathlon at Montreal this summer. *Damn, he's a handsome guy.* While eating breakfast I planned out my day. If I didn't hear from Paula or J.T. by the time I was ready to leave the house, I would head on over to Panta's Gym and get in a good workout and then check in with Dottie who was taking my calls. I was cleaning up the kitchen when the phone rang.

When I answered the phone, J.T. said, "I'll have you know this was a piece of cake."

"O.K.," I said.

"Got something to write with? I have a full report for you."

"Shoot," I said.

"Well, believe it or not, Reverend Malachi Jackson is a real sure-fire ordained minister. He grew up in a small town in Indiana and earned a theological degree from a seminary in Indianapolis."

"How did he end up in Texas?"

"Right out of the seminary he started a church in Hot Springs, Arkansas. He 'saved' a rich guy who had made millions betting on horses and the Church of the Chosen was born. He used his new disciple's connections and money to build a big sanctuary in Houston and from there it grew."

"How did you find this out?" I said.

"The man who donated those millions to the 'Chosen' lives here in Houston now. He has been a well-spring of information."

"Is he not with the 'Chosen' now?"

"That's an interesting story in itself, but here it is in a nutshell. The guy's name is Stan Chadwick and he said after Reverend Malachi Jackson brought several of his millionaire friends to the Lord and purged them of their money, the 'Chosen' left town and set up some kind of commune down in Mexico."

"That must have been about the time the Texas Rangers began investigating them."

"The Feds got after them as well, according to Stan."

"Stan?"

"Yeah, we got kinda chummy while I was there. He also said the Feds have been sniffin' around again lately trying to locate the 'Chosen'."

"Let me get this straight, the 'Chosen' pulled up shop, took the millions with them, and are living in a commune somewhere in Mexico."

"Yes," J.T. said.

"Who is living in the commune?"

"The Rev and about one hundred and fifty of his converts have been living at a compound outside a town called San Miguel in central Mexico. One of Jackson's VIP's is Sister Charlene. Stan's been there and has seen it."

"Why did he leave?"

"He had a falling out with the Rev and said he was lucky to get out. Stan said no one ever gets out."

"But they let him go?"

"He said the Rev swore him to secrecy and let him go because he owed him."

"Did he say anything about Kerry?"

"Not exactly, but he said there was a man they called the 'Protector' that fit Kerry's description."

"Do you think it's him?"

"My best guess is yes."

"Find out everything you can about that compound and get on up to Fort Worth as fast as you can."

"Why so fast?" J.T. asked.

"We're going to Mexico."

Chapter Thirty-seven

J.T. said he would be in Fort Worth by early evening. An attempt to call Paula again resulted in leaving another message. Panta Lopez was in the ring showing off his footwork when I walked into his gym. He glided across the canvas with flat punching mitts on his hands, making a welterweight he was training chase him around the ring. Panta moved his feet and his hands in unison barking out demands for the fighter to try harder.

"Come on, Chief, move your feet!"

The fighter threw an off balance punch, only hitting air.

"Move, move, move! Keep your balance and punch hard!"

I disappeared into the locker room and dressed out for my workout. Panta came in as I was going through my stretching regimen.

"Some guys came by here looking for you this morning."

"Who were they?" I said.

"Military, in uniform. There were three of them. One was an MP."

"They say what they wanted?"

"No, they said they would be back. You go AWOL or somethin'?"

"Remember? I was a war *hero*," I said, grinning. "If anything, they'd be giving me some kind of medal."

"Just thought you'd wanna know," Panta said. "Gotta go back to work."

The weight workout I put myself through over the next hour and a half was the stimulant I needed. Three rounds were spent on the speed bag and fifteen on the heavy bag. I was just about ready to lace up the gloves for a rematch with Sammy 'Upper Cut' Johnson, when the cavalry arrived. Three men in Air Force uniforms came into the gym and walked over to me.

"Mr. Cassidy," the Major said.

I noticed his Vietnam Service Medal.

"Yes sir," I said out of habit and respect.

"I am Major Benji Atchison." Looking at the men next to him, he said, "This is Lieutenant Anderson and Sergeant Billings of the U.S Air Force Military Police."

I nodded at them, but they gave no response.

"We need you to come with us," said Major Atchison.

"Do you mind if I ask why?"

The Major looked at the Sergeant.

"United States Congressman Sam McCullough would like to talk to you."

"O.K.," I said. "But why does it take three of you to ask me?"

This time Major Atchison looked at Lieutenant Anderson.

"It's military protocol, sir," the Lieutenant said.

"Military…protocol?"

"Yes, sir, Mr. Cassidy," Sergeant Billings said.

"Explain to me what that is," I said.

"Mr. Cassidy," Major Atchison said, "we heard you are stubborn sometimes."

"Who told you that?"

"Can't say," Lieutenant Anderson said.

"We know of your reputation as a boxer," Sergeant Billings said, "and wanted to make sure we had a sufficient number of men to convince you to come in with us."

"It's that important?" I said.

"Yes," the Major said. "It is to the Congressman."

Uncle Sam wants me…again.

Chapter Thirty-eight

Major Atchison, Lieutenant Anderson, and Sergeant Billings escorted me down a long hallway inside headquarters at Carswell Air Force Base northwest of downtown Fort Worth. The Major stopped me outside a door with a sign on it that read 'Briefing Room A'. He went inside and a few seconds later opened the door and motioned me into the room. It was dark except for a light coming from a slide projector. Major Atchison closed the door behind me and left the room. Three people sat looking at a map projected upon a large screen. A tall man sitting in the middle stood up and walked over to me.

"Mr. Cassidy," he said, "my name is Sam McCullough, United States Congressman from Houston. I think you know Miss Conn."

My eyes went quickly to Paula as she stood up in the light of the projector and smiled.

"Yes, I do." I smiled back at her and her eyes brightened.

"Mr. Cassidy…" the Congressman said.

"Please, call me Pat."

"O.K., Pat. Let's keep this on a first name basis since everything we're doing here is quite illegal and hush-hush, if you know what I mean. I'm Sam…and this fine gentleman is Buck."

The other person in the room stood up, turned around, and nodded at me.

"You are familiar with what Paula does," Sam said. "Buck is retired CIA and has been kind enough to help us with our plans."

"Plans?" I asked.

"Join me over here at the map and let me show you something."

We walked over to the slide projector where Paula nudged me with her left shoulder.

"It's good to see you," she whispered.

"You, too," I whispered back.

"This is the state of Guanajuato, Mexico," the Congressman said. "Do you see the city of San Miguel de Allende?"

"Yes." I walked to the screen and pointed to a spot on the map. "Outside San Miguel, the Church of the Chosen has a compound where they are holding constituents of your district against their will…and you want me to help you get them out."

Congressman McCullough turned to Paula and winked at her.

"He's as good as you said he was."

"Pat," Paula said, "when Sam told me what he was up to, we went over the intelligence report of the people involved and a name came up that I recognized right away. I knew you were looking for Kerry Vogel. His name was among the principals involved with the Church of the Chosen."

"Our investigation turned up the same information," I said. "What's your plan?"

Paula looked at the Congressman. The Congressman then looked at Buck.

"The CIA has a secret landing strip near San Miguel that the Mexicans don't know about. We used it to launch subversive missions to overthrow Central and South American dictators back in the sixties."

"The CIA still has trucks and other equipment stored there that we can use," Congressman McCullough added. "Once we get to the base, we'll take a truck to the 'Chosen's' compound, and I'll negotiate their release."

"Just like that," I said. "What are you going to negotiate with?"

"Money," the Congressman said.

"Congressman..."

"Please, call me Sam. Remember, first name basis from here on out."

Paula looked at me with a slight smile on her face.

"Sam," I said, "Reverend Malachi Jackson has all the money he'll ever need."

"He may have a lot of money, but I only want to get my people out of there and I believe we'll be able to negotiate a trade."

"Keep in mind they are a bit fanatical."

"I know they are, Pat," Sam said.

"If you are able to negotiate with the Rev, then you're in good shape, but you better be prepared for the worst in case they're as crazy as they seem."

"We're prepared, but there is one small problem."

"What's that?"

"We're having a problem getting clearance to fly a government plane on a secret mission into a foreign country."

"What about a privately owned plane?"

"That could be arranged if we could only find one. Up to this point, none of my constituents or financial backers are willing to take the risk."

"How many people do you plan on bringing back?"

"The four of us," Sam said, "and eight of my constituents."

"The five of us," Paula said, "don't forget about Shaggy, my cameraman."

"Oh, that's right," Sam said, "the five of us and my constituents."

"I have a friend coming that will want to be in on this, too, and I want to bring back Kerry Vogel."

"All right, Pat. So we need a plane that will bring back at least fifteen people."

"Let me make a phone call and I'll have one here in a couple of hours."

Sam looked at Paula. "He is good."

Chapter Thirty-nine

Sam provided a phone and I called Jeb Glasscock. He said his new Learjet 36A was in a hanger at the Brown County Airport and he could have it in Fort Worth right away. The only problem is the plane would only hold eight passengers. Sam and Buck were leaning over a conference table looking at a map and discussing the timing of the mission, when I walked back into the briefing room. Paula sat across from them taking notes in a reporter's notebook. The lights were on now, which allowed me to really appreciate her pretty face. Sam stood up erect and appeared taller and thinner than he had earlier in the darkened room. I'm six three and he was a good four inches taller than me. His angular face was highlighted by a pointed nose and his hair was dark brown and cut short. The Congressman wore a leather Air Force pilot's jacket with military issue khaki shirt, trousers, and boots. Buck was six feet with a thick solid body that probably got that way through a lot of hard work in the weight room. He looked every bit the old soldier with his blonde crew cut and olive drab army fatigues with no insignias. Buck's army pants were tucked inside his black patent leather combat boots that glimmered under the bright fluorescent lights.

"Jeb's Learjet will be here soon," I said. "There is only one problem."

"What's the problem?" Sam said with a worried look.

"It only carries eight passengers."

"Is it a Learjet 35?" Buck asked.

"No, Jeb said it was a 36A."

"That's the brand new model. Probably cost your boss a couple of mil. We'll be O.K. The 36A holds over three thousand pounds of cargo. We're taking about a thousand pounds and six additional passengers would be about another thousand pounds. The ride back will be a little crowded, but all we want to do is get those people out."

"I take it you're well versed with this type of plane," Paula said.

"Yes, ma'am," Buck said. "I was one of the first pilots to train to fly the C-21A. That's what the Air Force called the original Learjet 35. They've made a lot of improvements in the latest model, but they still fly the same. If I had to, I could fly us in and out of there without a problem."

"Let's hope it doesn't come to that," Sam said. "Pat, when is your colleague going to be here?"

I looked at my watch.

"J.T. will pull into Fort Worth in about an hour. I need to go get him and let him know what's going on."

"Not a good idea, Pat. I think we should all stay on base until we're ready to leave. Besides you are my liaison with Mr. Glasscock's pilots. Where is J.T. going to be?"

"I told him to meet me at WFTW or Ernie's Bar and Grill. They're right next door to each other downtown."

"How convenient," Sam said. "I will dispatch Major Atchison and his men to bring him in."

"By the way, Sam," I said. "When your men came to pick me up earlier today they told me they heard that I might be stubborn about coming in with them. Where did you get an idea like that?"

Sam grinned and motioned with his head toward Paula, still sitting at the table writing in her notebook. She stopped writing and looked up at me with a guilty look on her face.

"What? I was just telling him the truth."

Chapter Forty

Jeb's Learjet landed at Carswell Air Force Base late that afternoon and taxied onto the tarmac where Sam, Paula, and her cameraman sat waiting in one Jeep and Buck and I in another. The cameraman's real name was Simon Winkler, but everyone called him Shaggy. He pointed his camera at Jeb's Learjet and panned in our direction. Then Shaggy hopped out of the jeep with the camera on his right shoulder and filmed the Congressman and Paula gazing toward something as if it might save the world. A few minutes later Curtis Patterson, the pilot, and Ken Schultz, the co-pilot, exited the plane dressed in dark blue matching uniforms with silver wings above the left pockets. They both wore dark blue baseball caps with Jeb's international logo on the front. Curtis was carrying a briefcase. Sam, Paula, and I got out of our Jeeps and met them halfway across the tarmac. Buck stayed behind.

"Good to see you, Pat," Curtis said, shaking hands.

"How's the fishing at Lake Brownwood these days, Ken?" I said as we shook.

"Not too bad, Pat."

Curtis and Ken were always in attendance at Jeb's yearly deer hunt at the Glasscock Ranch and we had become acquainted through the years.

"Curtis, Ken, this is U.S. Congressman Sam McCullough from Houston."

They exchanged handshakes.

"This is Paula Conn…"

"We know who she is, Pat," Ken said, smiling.

They both enjoyed shaking Paula's hand.

"The guy pointing a camera at us is Simon Winkler," I said.

"Shaggy," Simon said, peering through the view finder without moving his head or the camera.

"Come this way, gentlemen," Sam said. "We're going to take you to the briefing room back at headquarters."

Curtis got in the Jeep with Sam and Paula. Ken followed me to the Jeep where Buck was waiting. Shaggy turned off his camera long enough to climb into the backseat of our jeep, and then began filming Sam, Paula, and Curtis driving away with the Learjet in the background.

"Ken Schultz," Ken said, introducing himself to Buck.

Buck nodded.

Sam had sandwiches and soft drinks brought in while we discussed the mission around the conference table. Shortly after seven o'clock the briefing room door swung open and in walked Major Atchison.

"Sorry we're late, Congressman."

Out of Touch

The Major had a blackened eye and his tie was crooked. A moment later Lieutenant Anderson and Sergeant Billings hauled J.T. into the room in handcuffs. The Lieutenant's nose had been bleeding and the Sergeant had a big red knot on his forehead.

"He was a handful, sir. He didn't want to come with us. It took all three of us to get him down on the ground in order to cuff him."

J.T., with arms behind his back, looked a little worse for the wear.

"Would someone tell me what in the hell is going on here?" J.T. shouted.

He started to say something else, but then he noticed Paula and closed his mouth. Then he saw me.

"Aw…Cassidy! What in the hell have you gotten me into now?"

"Take the cuffs off, Major," Sam said.

Major Atchison nodded at Sergeant Billings and he pulled a key out of his pocket and took off the handcuffs. J.T. rubbed his wrist and then made a flinching move at the Sergeant, who jumped back as if he was about to get punched again.

"We confiscated his weapon once we got him into handcuffs," the Major said, pulling J.T.'s shiny nickel-plated Smith and Wesson .44 Magnum out from under his uniform jacket.

"Give him his gun back," Sam ordered.

The Major held the gun by its eight and three-eighths inch barrel and handed it back to J.T. He grabbed the walnut grip and shoved it into the holster underneath his blue jean jacket.

"Thanks, Major," Sam said, dismissing the Major and his detail.

"Now," J.T. said, still a little huffy, "...will someone tell me what on God's green earth is going on here?"

"Have a seat, sir," Sam said.

"If you don't mind, I'd rather stand."

Chapter Forty-one

J.T. calmed down and took a seat at the conference table once he heard my explanation of why we were all there. Curtis and Buck described the flight plan, which included estimated times of separation and arrival.

"Pat, J.T. and I," Buck said, "will be supplied with M-16 rifles for defensive measures. However, if Sam is not able to negotiate a trade for his people, then we go in after them."

"J.T.," I said. "What did you find out about the compound?"

"Let me see the map," he said, reaching across the table and sliding it toward him.

"Buck," Sam said, "let's put the big map up on the screen."

Buck got up out his chair, turned the slide projector on and turned out the lights. J.T. studied the map for a moment and then pointed to an area near San Miguel.

"The compound is about ten miles southwest of San Miguel near Rio Laja and fortified by ten feet high rock walls that the 'Chosen' built after moving there some years ago."

"The CIA airstrip is northeast of San Miguel on a plateau surrounded by the Bajio Mountains," Buck added, showing us on the map. "The Agency closed it down because the area was becoming a tourist site. Gringos, both American and Canadian, have all of a sudden found the place interesting."

"Buck," Sam asked, "will we be able to bypass San Miguel to get to the compound?"

"Yes, there will be no need to go into San Miguel unless we want to."

"Hold it, Sam," Paula chimed in, "you promised me a night on the town."

"Yes, you'll get your night on the town," Sam conveyed to her, "but first things first."

"I'm going to hold you to that, Sam."

"Buck, run us through the plan from beginning to end," Sam said.

"We board the plane tomorrow at oh-seven hundred hours. The trip will take us about two hours. Once we secure the airstrip and barracks area, Pat and I will reconnoiter the compound. J.T. will stay with the rest of you for security reasons."

"We'll be flying into Mexican air space without authorization," I said. "The Federales are bound to know about it when we do."

"That has been taken care of," Sam said. "The Mexican oil fields aren't doing so well these days, thanks to our tinkering. The Mexican government is much more willing to accept a bribe to ignore us. However, you all need to know this…we have forty-eight hours to get this done or the Federales will descend upon us like locusts."

"We'll get the job done, Sam," Buck asserted. "When Pat and I get back from the compound we'll make our final preparations. At this point, our plan is to get a message to the Reverend Jackson that Sam wants to meet with him to broker a deal."

"How will we do that?" I said.

"Easy, Pat," Sam said. "I promised Paula a night in San Miguel de Allende. We go into a local cantina and talk a lot of trash about the 'Chosen' and how we're here to take back some Americans. They'll get the message, and before the night is up…a meeting will be arranged."

"You sure about that?" J.T. asked.

"The dollar goes a long way down there," Buck replied.

"I thought you were going to show me a night on the town just to be nice to me," Paula teased.

"A night on the town is a night on the town," Sam said. "We have a rare opportunity to enjoy ourselves while at the same time bring these people home. We'll be arriving there while a weeklong celebration called the Semana Santa is going on. It's the second most important holiday in Mexico. The children get two weeks off from school to enjoy elaborate reenactments of the twelve stages of the cross and passion plays. The night will be filled with fireworks and people, including tourists. It will make an appropriate cover for our presence. While this is going on, we'll have a good time and get word to Reverend Malachi Jackson that I want a meeting with him."

"Once the meeting is set," Buck said, "then Sam will negotiate with the Rev, Paula will work on her story, Pat will try to locate Kerry Vogel, and if everything goes as planned, everyone will return to the airstrip and we'll all go home. But just in case, J.T. and I will be waiting in the wings to come in and get you out if need be."

"The best laid plans of mice and men often go awry," I said.

"A poem by Robert Burns," Sam said. "'Ode to a Mouse'."

"You can talk all you want to about mice and men," J.T. interjected, "but the 'Chosen' ain't any Mickey Mouse organization. My man Stan, back in Houston, told me they're armed with Czechoslovakian manufactured assault rifles that are deadly accurate. These people are serious."

Let the fireworks begin!

Chapter Forty-two

Buck took J.T. and me to a hanger where he had collected the necessary supplies for 'Mission de Allende' as Sam had named our plans at the end of the briefing session.

"We are...that is we three...are dressing in black. Sam wants no olive drab or camo for this mission," Buck said. "But bring your civvies for the night in San Miguel."

"If we hit the compound and they see us dressed like soldiers they'll think there's an invasion," J.T. quipped.

His comment almost made Buck smile.

"If we're all dressed in black," I said, "we'll be able to ID each other and hopefully cut down on friendly fire...in case there is any shooting."

"Boots, long sleeve t-shirt, pants, watch cap, backpack, and light jacket," Buck said, "all black and courtesy of Uncle Sam."

"Black is beautiful," J.T. said, grinning.

"Is he always this way?" Buck said.

This time J.T.'s humor seemed to annoy Buck.

"The best I can tell," I said.

Buck picked up an M-16 rifle and tossed it to J.T. He caught it with both hands and immediately put the stock up against his shoulder aiming at an imaginary target somewhere on the other side of the hanger.

"Ever used one of these?" Buck asked.

"No, but it sure feels good holding it."

"The M-16A1," Buck said, "can be used as a full or semi-automatic weapon and fires a 5.56 millimeter bullet that will penetrate a helmet or flak jacket from three hundred yards. You'll be issued two hundred and fifty rounds."

"You expect a war to break out or something?" J.T. said.

"You have to be careful when burst-firing," I said. "The problem with the M-16, as with any burst-fire weapon, is they have a tendency to waste ammunition."

"Here, Pat," Buck said handing me a rifle. "Sam and I had a look at your service record. Say hello to an old friend."

The M-16 fit my hands like an old pair of gloves.

"The A/1/6," Buck said. "You guys were in some brutal fighting in Quang Tin back in '67 and '68. The Agency had me in Laos at the time…causing trouble."

"It's a time in my life I would rather forget."

"Do you ever see your old Sergeant…Finnegan O'Leary?" Buck said.

"You know the Sarge?" I said, a little surprised.

"I pay attention to men who win the Congressional Medal of Honor."

"I ran into the Sarge and his wife, Carmen, a few years back at a restaurant in Abilene. He's a rancher now."

"A real cowboy," Buck said.

"And a real hero," I said.

Buck nodded.

"Over there," Buck said pointing, "we have fifty gallons of gasoline in five gallon cans as a backup. When we abandoned the airstrip two years ago we secured our supplies, but you never know. We're also well supplied with military rations and water."

"Sounds like a plan," J.T. said.

"It's a good plan we believe. J.T., you have your .44, Pat carries a Browning nine millimeter, and I'll be armed with my new Beretta nine. As I said earlier, you'll be well supplied with ammunition for the M-16's, and we'll make sure you have plenty of ammunition for your personal weapons, too. We could be in for one hell of a battle before we can get those people out."

The hanger door slid open and Sam walked in carrying a bottle of Johnny Walker Black Label and four paper cups.

"Gentleman, I'm assuming you're all about ready for tomorrow's adventure and ready to get a good night of sleep."

"We're ready, Sam," Buck said with confidence.

"We'll all be staying in a barracks that I've had prepared for us and reveille is at five in the morning. Everyone take a cup and let's make a toast to our success."

Sam poured us each a full cup of scotch. We held them up in a toasting fashion.

"In preparing for battle," Sam said, "I have always found that plans are useless, but planning is indispensable."

Sam, Buck, and J.T. started to take a drink.

"General Dwight D. Eisenhower," I said.

"Very good," Sam said. "Now drink up."

Chapter Forty-three

The Learjet lifted off the runway at precisely seven o'clock in the morning and 'Mission de Allende' was officially underway. A few minutes later, Curtis announced we could remove our seatbelts. I took mine off and walked to a sitting area in the back of the plane. Paula joined me.

"You scared?" Paula said.

I just looked at her without speaking.

"Silly question to be asking you, but I'm scared to death."

"You'll be fine, Paula. We're not going to let anything happen to you."

"Thanks. Believe it or not, that makes me feel a little better about all this."

"Tell me about Shaggy," I said.

"Best cameraman in the biz," Paula said.

"Where did he get the name Shaggy?"

"Isn't it obvious? He looks like Shaggy from Scooby Doo."

I nodded, smiling.

"Shaggy is a hoot," Paula said. "I can't wait for you to get to know him better."

"How is life in the fast lane?" I asked.

"Exactly what I thought it would be."

"You happy?" I asked.

"The experience so far has been so fascinating," Paula said. "Exciting, exhilarating, and very fulfilling."

"It appears it agrees with you."

"It does, Pat...and I have you to thank for it."

"Paula, you don't need to thank me."

She stared at me with inquisitive blue eyes that looked like something right out of a fashion magazine. Her long red hair was rolled up in a bun and she was wearing a light brown safari jacket with tan slacks tucked into lace up boots that stopped just short of knees.

Paula started to say something else when Sam walked up and asked if he was interrupting anything.

"No, no, Sam," she said, "please, have a seat."

Sam glanced at Paula and flashed a smile that probably helped him get elected several times.

"Paula, would you excuse us for a moment? I would like to have a word with Pat."

"Sure," she said and got up out of her chair.

"Pat, I want you to do something for me," Sam said in an undertone.

"What's that?"

Sam surveyed the cabin to see if anyone was paying attention to us. Paula walked over and sat next to J.T. Buck sat motionless reading from a magazine. Shaggy was in the front seat of the cabin fiddling with his camera.

"I want you to kill Reverend Malachi Jackson."

Sam looked me square in the eyes. I met his stare with a deadpan glare.

"I'm not a hired assassin," I said.

"Look at it as doing the world a favor," Sam said.

"I'm not your man."

"Pat, being a United States Congressman and Chairman of the House Armed Services Committee, I have access to information that isn't available to everyone."

"Good for you."

"Yes, it is good for me. It makes me a very powerful man in Congress."

"Now that *is* very good for you."

"I've heard you can be a wisenheimer."

"Where did you hear that from…Paula?"

"No," Sam said as he uncrossed his legs and leaned toward me. "Private First Class Joe Haley."

"Congressman, spit it out. Don't play games with me."

"He testified under oath about some of your questionable actions at Tam Key."

"I was only following orders," I said.

"That's the only thing that saved you from a Court Martial."

"I did what the United States Army trained me do. Kill the enemy."

"Is what I have asked you to do any different than what you did in Vietnam?"

"Yes, Congressman, we're not at war."

"O.K., Pat, drop the Congressman and let's get back to a first name basis here. I understand you're angry at me for bringing this up, but if we don't do something about this man, those people in the compound will never get their lives back."

"I thought you were only interested in your eight constituents?"

"First, and foremost," Sam said, "however, a very wise and rich contributor of mine wants to see this weirdo put to rest."

"So, it's about money, then."

"Not exactly, he wants to see justice served. Reverend Malachi Jackson has stolen millions of dollars and done irreparable damage to their lives and their family's lives."

He has a point.

Sam leaned back in his chair and folded his hands together in his lap.

"Just like at Tam Key," Sam said. "If you cut off the head, the body dies. It's your call."

Chapter Forty-four

"We are approaching the airstrip," Curtis said through the cabin speakers. "Please buckle your seatbelts."

Buck got up and went into the cockpit. A few minutes later he returned to his seat and buckled up.

"Other than weeds growing on the runway, it looks fine," he said. "The landing will be a little bumpy, but we're in good shape."

We felt the plane bank to the right as Curtis circled the airstrip and then slowly descended for the landing. As we touched down, the landing was somewhat rough as Buck had promised. When the plane slowed to a stop, everyone appeared relieved.

"Pat," Buck said, "you and J.T. come with me."

Outside the plane and armed with M-16 rifles, we proceeded to a building about fifty yards from the runway. A few feet from the entrance Buck aimed his rifle at the latch on the front door and fired three shots until it fell off its hinges and the lock spiraled to the ground. He pushed his way through the door and J.T. and I followed. Buck took out a flashlight and maneuvered his way through the building, one room at a time, until he reached the generator. He took the cap off the fuel tank and sniffed it. Then he put his rifle down and grabbed a five gallon gas tank. It was empty, so he put it down and picked up another one.

"It's still full," he said, screwing off the lid.

Buck poured the gasoline into the generator and then pushed a button. The generator cranked up and lights began to slowly brighten. In a few minutes the entire building had electricity.

"American ingenuity," Buck said, grinning, "there's nothing like it."

In the garage sat an olive drab M54 military cargo transport truck and two Jeeps. Buck opened the hood of the M54 and connected battery cables to it from a wall unit that lit up and hummed as he turned it on. Then he took off the air filter cover and primed the carburetor.

"See if it will crank," he said to J.T.

J.T. climbed into the cab and pumped the accelerator about a half dozen times. The engine turned over a few times and stubbornly cranked up.

J.T. smiled widely and Buck gave us thumbs up.

In less than an hour we had unloaded our supplies, dusted off, and straightened up much of the area inside the building we would be using for our short stay at the Agency's abandoned secret base.

"How come the locals have never found this place?" Paula asked.

"They're superstitious about what they call the 'Bajio Demon'," Buck explained. "Some sort of cocky pock they believe in. If they see it, they'll lose their soul to the devil."

"What about from the air?" I questioned. "Why hasn't anyone spotted it?"

"The Agency took all that into consideration. There are no commercial airlines that fly anywhere near this place and the ones that do are at forty thousand feet. The airstrip is difficult to see from seven miles up and the Mexican Air Force is almost non-existent."

J.T. appearing a little perplexed, asked, "Don't they see the planes land?"

"San Miguel is blocked by the mountains," Buck continued, "and on the other side…more mountains. Plus, it's harder than hell to get up here."

"Sam?" Paula said. "Are you ready to do our first interview?"

"Why, yes. Excuse us gentlemen while Paula chronicles 'Mission de Allende' on film."

"Let's go outside," Paula said. "Shaggy has a spot set up where the lighting is perfect with the mountains in the background."

As Sam and Paula left the room, Buck said, "The Jeep should be charged up by now. We should be heading to the compound soon."

"Well," J.T. said, "I hope you guys have fun without me. Is there a radio or television set around this place?"

"A radio, back in the supply room," Buck said. "But unless you understand 'Espanola' it won't do you any good."

"Oh, yeah," J.T. said, thrown off balance. "I never thought about that."

"I'll get the Jeep and meet you out front," Buck said.

J.T. and I walked out front and stood nearby as Paula interviewed Sam. Shaggy had his 16mm camera on a tripod squinting through the view finder. Paula held a microphone in her left hand.

"Thank you, Congressman," she said, concluding the interview.

Paula pointed toward J.T. and me and Shaggy panned the camera slowly around in our direction.

"This rescue mission here in Mexico also has an interesting twist to it. These two gentlemen, Pat Cassidy on the right, and J.T. Lambert on the left, are here to find a man by the name of Kerry Vogel who disappeared eight years ago from a small town in west central Texas and is thought to be a member of the Church of the Chosen."

Paula dropped the microphone down to her side and made a cutting motion with her free hand in front of her neck. Shaggy turned off the camera.

"Thanks guys, you both look cute dressed in black."

Like J.T. says...black is *beautiful.*

Chapter Forty-five

Buck mounted a hardtop roof on the Jeep and we headed south down narrow, winding, rough roads through the sporadic groves of dry forests along the rocky hillside of the Bajio Mountains. The descent was physically challenging, but breathtaking, as the Mexican lowland below us became visible. It was as if you could see forever. The hills below us were dry, rocky and nearly barren of vegetation. The rock formations had unusual shapes and appeared to jut up out of the ground like worn monuments and statues weathered smooth by wind and erosion. The rocks were surrounded by bushes that begged for a drink of water. But among the rocks, dry forests, and barren terrain of the Bajio, there was an occasional Mexican cliff rose with its beautiful white lobed flower.

After what seemed like forever, we finally turned west on what Buck identified as Highway 110. There were no signs and the roadway was barely wide enough for one vehicle. Fortunately, we didn't meet another automobile until the highway widened near San Isidro. At San Ignacio we turned onto a little better roadway called Highway 57 and cruised for about another twenty kilometers. The landscape along the roadside was nearly as rugged as the mountains. Prickly cacti inundated the terra, some with purple flowers in bloom, others that Buck called Golden Barrel Cactus, stood as tall as five feet. There was an occasional Huizache Chino, a small sickly looking tree indigenous to this area of Mexico. The Yucca and other succulent plants looked commonplace in their environment adding color, and a spattering of hope, that one could actually survive here. Most of the natives lived in ordinary looking homes constructed of plain adobe bricks and native rocks sometimes painted brightly in shades of green, yellow-gold, light blues, orange, and rust. Suddenly, and out in the middle of nowhere, Buck veered hard onto Highway 1 and passed a couple of slow moving chicken trucks.

"Anyone ever tell you that you drive like a bat-out-of-hell?" I said.

"That's the way the locals drive, besides I didn't wanna get stuck behind those damn trucks. They stink like chicken shit!"

Buck passed a battered slow moving truck about ten kilometers outside of San Miguel. The old man driving waved as we flew past him. As San Miguel neared, I noticed a small building off to my right painted light blue. A sign in bright red letters read 'Antiguedades.' A couple of ancient farm wagons sat out front along with some other relics from days gone by.

"We'll skirt around the outside of San Miguel and then take Highway 51 until we reach Rio Laja Road."

"How did you get hooked up with Sam?" I said.

"He recruited me. Mainly because of my knowledge of the area and the fact that I was retired CIA."

"Why are you doing it?"

"Mostly because I'm bored, but he offered me a lot of money. Let me rephrase that…what Sam is offering me is a lot of dinero to me."

"Why are *you* doing this?" Buck asked.

"I wonder sometimes, but I gave my word and I'm going to see the job through."

"How does J.T. play into all this?"

"He and Kerry Vogel were best friends in high school."

"I heard something on the news about that governor's thing you were involved in. J.T. was in on that, too, wasn't he? You guys partners or somethin'?"

"Something like that," I said.

"You act like best friends."

I thought about the way that sounded.

"You know, Buck, I think you might be right."

As Highway 1 turned into Highway 51, Buck said, "I take it you and Paula used to be an item."

"No, nothing is going on between us. We're just friends."

"It's gotta be more than that."

Buck grinned. Glancing over at him I could tell he knew that wasn't quite the truth.

"O.K.," I said, "it's a little more than just friends."

"That's what I thought," Buck said, nudging me with his right elbow. "She is a damn good lookin' woman."

"That she is, Buck. How about you? You married?"

"Never found the time. Was married to the Agency, but as the old adage goes…had a woman in every port."

"How about here in San Miguel?"

"Yes…I…did," Buck said smiling. "She was French Canadian, down here trying to find her inner self. That kind of woman is always best in the sack."

"What happened to her?"

"She finally discovered her 'inner self' and went back to Canada."

We didn't say anything to each other for a while. Buck drove us back into the mountains east of the Church of the Chosen's commune, parking the Jeep behind a ridge. We kept low behind the rocks casing the compound through field glasses. The rocked fortress was almost directly below us in a sunken valley. Out beyond the compound the Rio Laja flowed in a southerly direction. A grove of pine and oak trees sat at the base of a foothill north of the compound. The fauna around the rock perimeter seemed to be thicker than we saw driving in; probably because of its location near the river.

"Geez," Buck said. "The place looks like the damn Alamo."

"Have you ever seen the Alamo?" I said.

"Saw the movie."

"I've seen the real Alamo, Buck, and this looks nothing like it."

"Then why do I get the feelin' the Mexican Army is about to attack?"

Chapter Forty-six

"The compound is approximately the length and width of five football fields with two ways in and two ways out."

Buck stood next to a topographic map resting on a tripod. He had drawn a small square on the map to represent how the compound fit with the surrounding terrain.

"A main gate on the south side accesses Rio Laja Road and there is a smaller gate on the east side of the fortress wall facing the river. Inside the compound there is a series of small buildings interconnected by walkways. Pat and I think this is probably Reverend Jackson's main headquarters and possibly his living quarters. A dozen two-story barracks sit side by side on the south end near the main entrance, and a large garden area takes up most of the north side of the compound. These people are pretty self-sufficient. They've drilled their own well, tapping into the aquifer for a water supply, which wasn't an easy task considering they're living on a plateau. They appear to have a sewer system that purifies itself before dumping into the Rio Laja a hundred yards downstream."

"Ingenious," Sam said.

"Are they armed like we heard?" J.T. asked.

"Yes, they are," I said, leaning against the back wall of the room. "Czechoslovakian made Bren Guns, just like you said. These rifles were the British Army's principle light support weapon just until a few years ago."

Buck drew a large square on the face of the map with a black marks-a-lot and pointed at it.

"Two armed guards patrol each quadrant of the wall along a walkway that goes all the way around the inside of the compound. From our vantage point on the ridge above, we could have picked them off one at a time."

"Curtis," Sam said. "Buck will radio you when we've made the exchange and we're on our way back. Have your engines revved up and ready to go."

"I will, Congressman. Ken and I will get you out of here and back to Texas safe and sound."

"In case you're all wondering why we're really here," Sam said, "I want to read something to you." He took a folded sheet of paper out of his shirt pocket and unfolded it. "This letter was smuggled out of the compound a few months ago and mailed to me. It's from a man who lived in my congressional district all his life. He worked hard, saved his money, invested well and had a nice little fortune set aside for his retirement."

Sam got up out of his chair and stood in front of the map.

"*Dear Congressman McCullough, I'm writing this letter to let you know that I am being held against my will by the Church of the Chosen in a compound near San Miguel de Allende, Mexico.*"

The room became still as if we were in a vacuum. Sam looked up and then continued.

"I was once a faithful member and proud to be one of the Chosen. The Reverend Malachi Jackson delivered me to the Lord and I thought I had assured myself a place alongside Jesus when I purged myself of all worldly possessions and donated them to the Church. In doing so, I wholeheartedly joined the Chosen's pilgrimage to Mexico. But since I have been here I have witnessed disturbing changes. People are no longer able to speak their mind or have any say so on how our community is run. Some followers who have spoken up have mysteriously died or disappeared. We have witnessed corporal punishment personally carried out by Reverend Jackson. We have also seen men come to our community that some say must be Mexican drug smugglers. No one knows for sure because we are too frightened to speak about it among ourselves, never knowing if there are spies among us. But the belief between some of the trusted brethren is that Reverend Jackson is possibly financing drug cartels in the area. I asked to be released so I may return home to Houston with my wife and see our children again. The Reverend told me if I mention it again I would be dealt with harshly. So, now, I am a prisoner of the Church of the Chosen. Listed on the back of this letter are the names of seven other people, including my wife, who lived in your congressional district. Please bring us home. Sincerely, signed Walter L. Davis."

"Now, if everyone is ready," Sam said as he scanned our faces, "let's load up and head to San Miguel."

Chapter Forty-seven

Paula was dressed in a soft polyester long sleeve emerald dress that dipped in a V shape with fringe to her thirty-four bust line and gathered around her narrow waist. Her red hair dangled across her shoulders and was parted down the middle. A gold locket rested just above her firm cleavage, which J.T. and I couldn't help but notice, as she walked into the cantina of Hotel El Atascadero. If she was wearing shoes we didn't notice. What I did notice was the natural look of her makeup. She sat at the bar next to me and got the attention of the bartender with a wave of her hand.

"I'll have what they're drinking," Paula said.

"We're drinking Mexican tequila and beer," I said.

"Then so am I."

"Think you can handle it?" J.T. said.

"I can handle anything you can."

Paula smiled and turned toward us on her barstool. I took a sip of my Bohemia beer when I caught a whiff of her perfume. If the fragrance had not made her more attractive than she already was I would not have said anything, but it was like a magnet.

"Your perfume is…I don't know how to describe it, Paula," I said. "What is it?"

"A friend of mine in New York gave me a sample last week. It's a new fragrance called 'Oscar' from Oscar de la Renta."

"The clothes designer?" J.T. said.

"You know about Oscar de la Renta?" Paula said.

"I read People Magazine," J.T. quipped in response.

The bartender, named Alejandro, placed a bottle of Bohemia beer in front of Paula and poured a shot of Sauza Tequila into a shot glass with salt around the brim. He then slid a saucer next to the shot glass with several slices of lime.

"How did you know what kind of beer and tequila to order?" Paula asked.

"We just ordered beer and tequila," J.T. said.

"That's a novel approach."

"When in Rome," I said, "do as the Roman's do."

The bright yellow-gold wall behind the bar outlined the dark wood liquor cabinet with some bottles of liquor that we didn't recognize. Alejandro was dressed in a short sleeve black shirt with 'Hotel El Atascadero' written in aqua blue above the left pocket. At six feet tall, he was handsome with grayish hair and a mustache, reminding me of Cesar Romero. Lush hanging vines decorated the bar above our heads and beautiful Purshia Mexicana bushes lined the rock wall along the outside patio. The lighting was low inside the cantina and mostly tourists filled the tables. I glanced over my left shoulder and noticed a band unpacking their instruments on a small stage. Paula picked up her shot glass, licked the salt around the brim and held it up in a saluting gesture.

"Bottoms up," she said.

Paula swallowed the tequila and picked up her beer, chasing away the sting with a healthy swig.

"I'll bet you guys didn't think I could do it…did you?" Paula said with her eyes a little teary from the tequila shot.

"Another shot?" Alejandro said, holding the bottle of Sauza up in front us.

"Hell, yeah," J.T. said. "What was that you said, Pat, about the Romans?"

I nodded at Alejandro.

"Gentlemen," Paula said, "here we are on the threshold of another great story."

"Don't you find it interesting," J.T. said, "that fate keeps throwing us together in unusual and dangerous situations?"

I stopped admiring Paula's beauty and turned to look at J.T.

"How much tequila have you had?" I said.

"I have an introspective side," J.T. said, "and I haven't had any more than you."

Smiling, I sucked on a lime, licked the salt around the brim of the glass, downed another shot, and finished off the Bohemia.

The band began to warm up their instruments. A saxophonist belted out of tune sounds that eventually resembled something like music. The guitarist strummed a few chords hitting a high Brazilian beat.

"Paula," J.T. said, "Mr. Cassidy, here, ran into some really bad dudes when he was poking around in Austin asking questions about the 'Chosen.'"

"Let me guess," Paula said, "the 'bad dudes' got the worse end of the deal."

"Killed one of them," J.T. said. "Shot and apprehended the other one."

Paula took a drink of beer and Alejandro brought me a fresh one.

"Tell me about it," Paula said.

I did.

"Between what happened to Pat in Austin and what I found out in Houston," J.T. said, "we're pretty sure the Rev is mixed up with some kind of drug cartel."

"Which makes the 'Chosen' even more dangerous than we expected," Paula said.

"It is going to be very difficult to get those people out of the compound," I said, turning toward Paula who seemed to be sitting closer to me than she had earlier.

"Alejandro," Paula said with a sexy tone in her voice as if she was playing a role in a movie, "I'll have another shot."

"Will you guys excuse me?" J.T. said. His eyes were fixed on a beautiful Mexican woman sitting at the end of the bar.

He got up and walked down to the end of the bar and began talking to her. Whatever the language barrier might be between them, J.T. was resourceful enough to overcome it. They shook hands and J.T. sat down next to her. In the meantime, Paula took another tequila shot and drank some more beer.

"That does it for me," Paula said, "at least until after dinner."

"Where are we eating?" I asked.

"Bugambilia, somewhere up on El Jardin."

"What is El Jardin?" I said.

"The town square not far from here."

"Where is Sam tonight?"

"He's with Buck planning strategy. Sam said they would join us later this evening."

I drank some beer with my attention firmly fixed on Paula as she watched J.T. enjoy himself with the new friend a few feet away. She turned quickly to say something and caught my eyes riveted on her.

"You know we have some unfinished business, don't you?" Paula said, soaking up the blush of the moment.

"Yes, we do," I said. "By the way, Dad is the new Chief of Police in Fort Worth, or will be in a few days."

"Your father is going to be the new Chief?"

"Yes."

"That's a big story," she said, inquisitively.

"Paula, you can only do one story at a time."

"When we get back and this story runs its course, I'll jump on that one."

"Let's go out on the patio," I said.

The night sounds of San Miguel washed away the chattering and off-tune music inside the cantina. The sixteenth century colonial architecture lining the street made me feel as if I was back in time hundreds of years ago. The street climbed upward along a hill to the north, where the remaining sunset cast a brilliant display of colors that Pablo Picasso may have envisioned in one of his paintings. Fireworks shot upward from El Jardin lighting the night sky with brilliant colors. On the other side of the patio wall, we could hear voices from the crowded narrow street.

"That was really good the way you changed the subject at the bar," Paula said, standing in front me.

Exploding fireworks cast an array of colors that reflected across her face in the dim light on the patio. Each burst seemed to feature a different aspect of Paula's beauty.

"It wasn't on purpose," I said. "I was actually thinking the same thing. It's just when you brought it up, I thought about the two days we spent together at the lake. Dad being there put a cramp on things."

"To say the least," Paula said, "but I love Emmett and am very happy for him. Besides, we're here now."

I touched the side of her face and let my finger tips drift down the soft skin of her neck and stop to touch the gold locket.

"Beautiful locket," I said.

A couple sitting across the patio was watching us, so I slowly took my hand away and drank some beer from the bottle in my other hand. Paula looked around at the couple and then took a drink of her beer.

The different colors from another burst of fireworks reflected in Paula's blue eyes. We listened to the sound of the celebration of Semana Santa going on in the street on the other side of the rock wall. As the night grew cooler in San Miguel, the evening began to warm.

Chapter Forty-eight

Paula and I left J.T. with his new friend, Consuela, at the hotel and walked to El Jardin. The narrow street, Diaz de Soliano, paved with flat, worn-smooth rocks, climbed steeply upward. As we made our way through the mass of people we could see the neo-gothic tower of the Parroquia de San Miguel Archangel reaching toward the heavens. The lighting accentuated the baroque-style towers and made you feel that God really did live there. The architecture of San Miguel de Allende predated the eighteenth century, but with the celebration of Semana Santa, was being born again.

Two elderly men wearing wide brim straw cowboy hats stood by a doorway strumming guitars serenading the slow moving crowd. A half a block up Diaz de Soliano, we stopped to look in a window as a woman basted whole chickens in a manually turned rotisserie brick fired oven. The street vendors were selling everything from hand woven bags and hats to fresh fruit and vegetables in front of iridescent buildings. Yellow, brown, an occasional orange sherbet, and bright pink walls featured stately iron railed windows and balconies, while some of the windows at street level were covered with protective, but beautifully designed iron bars. Mexican flags were draped across second story balconies jutting out over the street. Pennants zigzagged from one side of the street to the other in a spectrum of different colors.

Crossing Cuadrante Street a block from El Jardin, the crowd bottlenecked in front of Bar San Miguel. The cantina sat cattycornered with old saloon-style swinging doors accessing both streets with its outside walls of pink and rust, chipped and faded.

"We have to go in and have at least one drink," Paula said with a mischievous smile.

Taking Paula's hand in mine, we managed to find a path to one of the saloon doors and then made our way into the packed cantina. We squeezed in close to each other at the bar. One of the bartenders quickly noticed Paula and brought us a round of beer and tequila.

"Do you think J.T. will make it for dinner?" Paula asked.

"It doesn't look that way," I said, looking around the place.

A mural of El Jardin during a different time in history was painted on the wall across the barroom. The bar itself had dark wood stain and was scuffed along the woodwork near the red tile floor. All the tables were full and domino games were being played at tables on the opposite end of the barroom. It was a loud, smoky and dirty place, but it gave the evening a new ambience.

"Unless Sam and Buck resurface," I said, "it'll be just you and me this evening."

Paula smiled and said, "They'll show, but that wouldn't be such a terrible thing."

She took a small sip from her shot glass and an even smaller sip from the beer.

Out of Touch

"I've had my drink in here now," Paula said. "Let's go...I don't like some of the looks I'm getting in this place."

I drank my shot of tequila and sipped a little of the beer and led Paula out of the bar. Once we reached El Jardin, it didn't take us long to discover Bugambilia's wasn't on the town square. But we asked around and made our way to Hidalgo Street a couple of blocks away to where it was located. Paula didn't want to sit around at the restaurant waiting for the rest of 'Mission de Allende' to arrive, so we left a message with the maitre d' that we would be down the street enjoying a Mariachi band. The band was playing at a cozy little bar called El Caporal that had a canopied patio dance floor. Paula was in such hurry to get back to the place, she almost dragged me down the street.

"I love Mariachi music," she said with excitement in her eyes. "Find us a table and order me a beer. I'll be right back."

Paula made her way to the ladies' room and I settled into a corner table for two with a good view of the dance floor. The waitress brought two beers and sat them down on the small round table. I had just picked up my beer, when I noticed a man enter the bar and walk toward me. He was wearing all white and his clothes fit loose like pajamas. The man walked up and peered down at me.

"Are you Pat Cassidy?" he said.

"Yes," I said, taking a drink of the beer.

"I'm Kerry Vogel."

Looking at his full bearded face...I said, "That you are."

Chapter Forty-nine

Kerry and I stood talking when Paula returned from the ladies' room. She looked more beautiful than ever after redoing her hair and applying new makeup.

"What's going on?" Paula said, smiling at first, and then frowning as she sensed the tension of the moment.

"Paula Conn," I said. "Meet Kerry Vogel."

She nodded at him with raised eyebrows, unable to say anything.

"Do you mind, Paula? Kerry and I need to talk."

"That's O.K., Pat. I'll meet you back at the restaurant."

She left the bar across the dance floor.

"Can we leave this place," Kerry said, "and go somewhere else and talk?"

I nodded and followed him onto Hidalgo Street.

"I heard you were looking for me," Kerry said, scanning the faces around us.

"How did you find out?"

"Reverend Jackson told me. We've been anticipating your arrival."

"How did he know?" I said.

"Let's keep moving, Pat."

Kerry walked in the direction of El Jardin.

"Can you tell me something?" Kerry said.

"Sure, what would you like to know?"

"Who are you?"

"I work for Jeb Glasscock," I said.

"That makes sense," Kerry said, "it would take someone with Jeb's resources to find me."

Kerry flinched as a loud boom announced a new round of fireworks. The people crowded into the street stopped and looked up at another brilliant display of lights. We kept walking.

"Who is Sister Charlene?" I asked.

He stopped and looked at me.

"Charlie is my wife," Kerry said, and then began making his way through the horde of revelers.

"What made you disappear?" I said.

"Because…that's what Reverend Jackson said I was supposed to do."

"Can we back up here, Kerry? How did you go from being the quarterback of the future for U.T. to where you are today?"

"All in due time," Kerry said. "There is something I want you to do for me."

"What's that?"

"I want you to get my wife and son out of here and back to the states."

"You have a son?"

"Yes. Luke is four years old."

"Why do you want me to get your wife and son out of the compound?"

"The Kingdom," Kerry said.

"You call the compound your Kingdom?"

"Yes...and things are not what we thought they would be."

"Because Reverend Jackson is using the money he's bilked to finance drug smuggling."

Kerry nodded.

"I'm here with a United States Congressman who also wants to get some of his people out of your compound."

Kerry stopped.

"That could be arranged," he said, "if you promise me you can get my wife and son out."

"What about you?" I said.

"I don't know if that's possible."

"Why?"

"My job is the day to day operation of the Kingdom and to protect it from invasion and outside influences."

"Will you come back with your wife and child if I can get you out?"

"Pat, I just don't know if that's possible."

"Sheriff Vogel misses you terribly," I said.

"Dad is still the sheriff?"

He seemed pleased to hear the news. We continued to make our way through the crowd.

"Give me the names of your congressman's people and I'll arrange to have them on a work detail that will put them outside the...," Kerry thought for a moment and then said, "compound."

"By the way, Kerry," I said. "J.T. is here to help get you out."

Kerry stopped and grinned from ear to ear.

"Where is he? I want to see him."

"You'll get your chance if you'll let me take you back with the others."

"Just promise me you'll get Charlie and Luke away from here."

"You have my word, but I'm bringing you back, as well. I gave my word to your dad."

There's a price to pay for every promise.

Chapter Fifty

When Kerry Vogel and I walked into Bugambilia's, J.T. was sitting next to Consuela having a good time. He glanced at me and grinned ready to make a smart aleck remark, when he saw Kerry. His mouth dropped open when he realized who he was. Obviously, Paula had not broken the news that I had found him. *Or, he had found me.* J.T. walked over to him and they stood eye to eye before grabbing each other with a bear hug. Paula, Sam, Buck, and Shaggy sat at the table watching. Kerry and J.T. broke their grasp on each other with solid slaps on the side of their arms, fighting back tears. It was an emotional reunion.

"Come have a seat, Kerry," J.T. said. "There is so much I need to ask you."

"It'll have to wait, J.T.," I said, "Kerry will need to return to the compound soon and we have a lot of planning to do before tomorrow."

Sam stood up and introduced himself.

"I'm Sam McCullough, United States Congressman from Texas."

They shook hands.

"I can help you get your people out," Kerry said.

"Good," Sam said. "That's exactly what I wanted to hear."

'Mission de Allende', plus Kerry, left the restaurant and reconvened in a conference room at Hotel El Atascadero. J.T., the gentleman, returned Consuelo to the bar before joining us. Shaggy stood in the corner of the room with his camera documenting the moment. Paula took notes as we discussed our plan to free Sam's constituents and the Kerry Vogel family.

"Tomorrow morning after the first meal," Kerry said, "I will lead a work detail through the gate on the side of the Rio Laja. There may be a problem changing the work detail first thing in the morning. Reverend Jackson may question some of my changes."

"We'll have to deal with that as it happens," I said. "I'm assuming you'll have your wife and son with you."

"I will," Kerry said. "I'll take the detail to the edge of the river where we have a second produce garden planted and a compost site we use for fertilization. They'll pull weeds, irrigate the garden, and dump yesterday's food waste."

"That's when J.T. shows up in the boat," Buck said, "and Kerry gets everyone loaded as quickly as possible."

J.T.'s eyes were fixed on Kerry, but nodded, affirming he had heard Buck.

"There may be confusion among your people, Congressman," Kerry said, looking at Sam.

"We're on a first name basis for this mission, Kerry," Sam said. "Please call me Sam."

Kerry nodded.

"I'm not telling anyone about our plan, not even my wife. When J.T. arrives in the boat they may be frightened and not understand."

"That's why I'll be with him in the boat," Sam said. "They'll recognize me."

"You sure you want to put yourself in harm's way?" I said.

"I'll be fine," Sam said. "I've come this far and I want to be there when Walter and the others escape."

"Pat," Buck said, "you and I'll be up in the rocks on the ridge to the east of the river overlooking the compound. We'll be able to keep anyone from coming out of the gate after them with M-16 fire."

"What about us?" Paula said. "Where will Shaggy and I be?"

"You'll have the best seat in the house," Buck said. "Right next Pat and me."

"I don't like that arrangement," Shaggy said to Sam from behind the view finder of his camera.

"You promised me total access to everything," Paula said. "I want to be in the boat when everything happens."

"We can't, Paula," Sam said. "The only boat we could come up with on such short notice will hold ten people safely. As it is, we'll already have thirteen people on board when we shove off. We can't put two additional people in the boat."

"One, then. One more won't make a difference," Paula said firmly.

"It might," Buck said.

"Make room for Shaggy," Paula said. "We've got to have close up film of the rescue."

"O.K., Paula," Sam said. "Shaggy can come aboard."

"Where will the boat take us?" Kerry asked.

"To a place on the river about a mile south of the compound," Buck said, "where our transport truck will be waiting to take us to the plane."

"In the morning, gentlemen," Kerry said standing up to announce his departure, "and ma'am, of course. May God be with us."

Chapter Fifty-one

Early the next morning, Shaggy was smoking a cigarette leaning against the Jeep parked in front of the hotel. He was tall and lanky and I noticed his hand shook as he took a drag off his cigarette. Nearby, Buck spoke Spanish to a very short Mexican man with black hair slicked back and wearing a seersucker suit with a sky blue shirt open at the collar. Buck pulled an envelope out of his back pocket and counted the money inside it before handing it to the man. Sam and Paula, dressed much the way they were on the plane, exited the hotel through the front door in serious conversation. J.T. pulled up in the M54 transport and parked behind the Jeep.

"I've never been this nervous before," Shaggy said.

"Even more nervous than the first time you met Paula?" I said.

Shaggy's laugh was tense as he flipped his cigarette into the street and exhaled the smoke through his teeth. He had on a wrinkled light green t-shirt, faded bellbottom blue jeans, and gray tennis shoes. Some of the writing across the heart of the t-shirt was worn away but you could tell it still said, "Certified Member of the Silent Majority."

"You nervous, Pat?"

I studied his face and could tell the anticipation was really bothering him.

"Of course I am," I said. "We're all apprehensive about what's going down today."

"I grew up on a farm outside Des Moines, Iowa," Shaggy said. "The most danger I ever saw growing up were floods."

"But now you live in New York, Shaggy. It doesn't frighten you to ride on the New York City Subway?"

"Yeah," Shaggy said, smiling. "It's pretty scary sometimes. It really just depends on what time of day you're riding."

"Maybe it's like today," I said, "nothing really to get worked up about."

Shaggy made a head bob of some sort like he agreed with me. He appeared to be getting a grasp on his emotions.

Buck joined Sam and Paula and said something to them.

"How long you been with the network?" I asked Shaggy.

"A year," he said. "This is the biggest story I've ever covered. Paula personally picked me for this assignment."

"You must be pretty good at your work, then," I said.

Shaggy shrugged and reached for a styrofoam cup of coffee sitting on the hood of the Jeep and took a drink.

Sam waved Shaggy and me over. J.T got out of the transport and joined us.

"Buck tells me the boat has been procured and will be waiting for us when we arrive at the Rio Laja."

"Pat," Buck said, "I've mounted scopes on the M-16's. We'll be able to pick off a flea crawling on the compound wall."

"Could come in handy," I said.

He nodded and smiled broadly about the possibilities.

"When we get my people out," Sam said, "we'll load them up in the transport and head back to the base."

"When we get your people *and* Kerry and his family out," I said.

"Exactly," Sam said.

"What kind of boat are we using for the getaway?" J.T. asked.

"It's not really a boat, per se," Buck said. "It's a barge with two one-hundred fifty horsepower outboard motors. Even with everyone on board, it'll do the job."

"*If* you can keep the 'Chosen' from shooting at us," J.T. said.

"We'll do our best," Buck said.

"Just make sure Cassidy has a gun in his hand," J.T. said.

"Hear that?" Buck said, grinning at me. "Your partner is countin' on you to cover his ass."

"He's also the best shot I've ever seen," J.T. added.

I nodded, reassuring J.T. I wouldn't let him down.

"Once we load up in the transport," Sam said, "Buck and Pat will cover our rear, and if we're separated for any reason, we'll rendezvous back at the airfield. We should be good to go and back at Carswell by the middle of the afternoon."

Out of Touch

"Keep your heads down when the shooting starts," Buck said. "Also, make sure our people keep their heads down, as well. Pat and I will be up on the east ridge providing cover fire."

"Buck's right," Sam said. "The entire purpose of this mission is to get my people home in one piece."

"What about the rest of us?" J.T. asked.

"Collateral damage is always a part of the game," Sam said.

"No one is going to die," Buck said. "Not on my watch."

From your lips to God's ears.

Chapter Fifty-two

Buck's contact was waiting for us with the barge at a predetermined location north of the 'Chosen's' compound. J.T., Sam, and Shaggy floated out onto the river as the camera captured the moment. Paula and I followed Buck in the Jeep as he drove the M54 transport a little farther north before crossing a bridge to the east side of the river. Our caravan turned south on a road that ran along a rocky ridge butting up against the east bank of the Rio Laja. A mile south of the rocked fortress, we parked the truck in a rugged, but relatively flat area along the east bank. Buck climbed into the back of the Jeep and we retraced the path that would take us back into the hills. Buck and I were dressed in military issue black. We each had on shoulder straps with our personal weapons holstered underneath our left arms. Buck's weapon was a new Italian made Beretta nine millimeter. Through the rearview mirror, I watched him pull his semiautomatic out of its holster, load a round into the chamber, slip on the safety, and return it to its holster. Bouncing up a rugged trail, we reached our vantage point facing the compound across the river. Buck checked the M-16 rifles to make sure they were loaded and ready to fire. I pulled over near the apex of a ridge and parked the Jeep. We made our way to the top of the hill and found a position giving us a clear shot at the compound. Buck and I focused our scopes and used field glasses to keep an eye on the front gate, as Paula perched next to me on her knees.

"You think this is going to work?" she asked.

"It'll work," Buck said.

"What makes you so sure?" Paula needled.

I kept my eyes on the activity along the top of the east wall. Two young men casually moved along the walkway with their assault weapons slung over their right shoulders. They were both dressed in much the same fashion that Kerry had been dressed the night before. One had bushy dark hair with his bangs held back by a white sweat band and the other had long straight blonde hair down to the middle of his back.

"Those guys down there totin' the Brens don't really know how to use'em," Buck said.

"How do you know that?" Paula said.

"Pat's boy, Kerry. He told us last night they're not mercenaries. They're Jesus freaks."

"They have the rifles for intimidation," I said, pulling the field glasses away from my eyes and glancing at Paula. "More than anything else they brandish the weapons to scare people away."

"If they point them at us," Paula said and then corrected herself. "If they point them at Sam's people and shoot at them, they might get lucky."

"That may be the case, Paula, but they'll play hell when they do," Buck said. "Pat and I will pick'em off one at a time."

"Kerry's group is coming out," I said, looking through the glasses.

Buck focused his binoculars on the east gate as it swung open. A black Volkswagen slowly drove out of the compound pulling a small trailer with a 55 gallon barrel sitting in the middle of it. Five men and three women all dressed in white followed behind it, carrying hoes, rakes, and shovels. The Volkswagen crept to the edge of the river and stopped as Sam's constituents spread out across the garden and went to work. Two of the men picked up the barrel and dumped it in the compost pile, a few feet away. Kerry got out on the driver's side of the 'Beetle' and a tall beautiful blonde exited the passenger side. *That's got to be Charlie.* Then, a young boy bounced out of the backseat of the car and ran to the water's edge where he began throwing rocks into the river. *That's got to be Luke.*

"The boat's coming," Buck said, pointing up the river.

The sound of the outboards grew louder the closer the barge got to the work detail. Some of the 'Chosen' stopped working and looked in the direction of the noise. J.T. drove the barge toward them at a high rate of speed. Two of the workers dropped their tools and began running back toward the compound. J.T. shifted the outboards into neutral and trimmed the motors as he floated the barge near the shoreline. Kerry picked Luke up in his arms and grabbed Charlie by the arm pulling her toward the boat.

"Stop," Sam shouted, standing in the middle of the barge. "I'm United States Congressman Sam McCullough and I'm here to take you home."

The two 'Chosen' that had turned to run back in the direction of the compound, did an about face, and ran as fast they could toward the boat. The others still in the garden began running across the rows of growing produce and splashed into the water. Kerry tossed Luke into the arms of J.T. and helped Charlie into the barge as he stood in the shallow water. Buck and I watched everything unfold below us and scanned the east walkway of the compound through the scopes of our rifles.

"We have activity along the wall," Buck said.

"I see it, Buck. If anyone raises a rifle, take'em out."

Kerry was helping his fellow 'Chosen' into the barge when a guard along the walkway took aim at his back.

"I've got'em," Buck said. "He's in my cross hairs."

Buck pulled the trigger and the toy soldier disappeared behind the top of the wall.

"They're almost all on board," I said.

"Got another one, Pat."

Focusing on the top of the wall through the scope I saw the guard with a headband aim his Bren. A second later, Buck shot him in the shoulder and the shooter dropped his weapon wincing in pain.

"They're all on board!" Paula shouted, standing up.

I was down on a knee when I reached up and yanked Paula's left arm so hard I lost my balance and she fell on top of me. We were eye to eye as a tantalizing curl of red hair pulled loose from her 'updo' and brushed across my face.

"Why, Mr. Cassidy," Paula said with a teasing smile, "I didn't think you cared."

"Stay down or you'll get yourself killed," I said.

"Will you two love birds quit playing around over there!" Buck shouted. "They're away!"

Paula climbed off of me and readjusted her clothes.

Shaggy stood calmly filming the rescue from the front of the barge as J.T. navigated them out of harm's way. Buck and I looked at each other believing the mission was accomplished. We were wrong. Reverend Malachi Jackson and two of his armed guards ushered twelve followers out the east gate of the compound and ordered them down, side by side, on their knees. The Rev was not at all what I had expected to see. What I expected to see was a man of God, despite everything we had found out about him. Instead, we were looking at a big, strong man who at the moment appeared to be angry. Reverend Jackson had a megaphone in one hand and a revolver in the other.

Speaking through the megaphone he said, "WHOEVER YOU ARE THAT HAS TAKEN AWAY MY BRETHREN. YOU ARE RESPONSIBLE FOR THIS."

Then he put the barrel of his gun against the back of the head of the nearest 'Chosen' and pulled the trigger. The body jolted forward and fell, lifeless.

"He's going to kill them all!" Paula screamed.

"You take him out, Pat," Buck said. "After all…you were good at that kind of thing in Vietnam."

Reverend Jackson pointed his revolver at the back of the head of another follower. Focusing the cross hairs of the scope on the middle of his forehead, I squeezed the trigger.

Chapter Fifty-three

Buck…driving like Buck…caught up with the M54 transport before it reached Highway 51. J.T. pulled the truck over and we informed Sam that Reverend Jackson was dead. Sam went to the back of the transport and informed Kerry.

"I wish I could say I'm sorry," he said, jumping down from the back of the truck. "There are many good men among the brethren that will do the right thing and if anyone wants to go home they'll be able to now. However, there will be those who want to stay. Especially since Reverend Jackson is dead. There could even be a power struggle."

"What about you?" J.T. said.

"The 'Chosen' will do fine without Charlie and me."

J.T. nodded.

"Let's get to the airstrip and go home," Sam said. "'Mission de Allende' is complete."

Famous last words.

Curtis and Ken smoothly lifted off from the airstrip with the weight of eleven additional passengers. The former 'Chosen' would now return to being United States citizens and happy constituents of Sam McCullough's congressional district. In the meantime, they were taking up every available space in the cabin. Kerry, J.T., Paula, and I squeezed into the small sitting area in the back of the plane. Sam, who had taken a liking to Charlie, sat next to her in the two luxury seats that were swiveled around to face us. Luke was asleep on a makeshift bed near his mother.

"What now, Kerry?" I asked.

"We go back and try to put this behind us. Start anew."

"It may be harder than you think," I said. "Charlene could be facing charges in Harris County."

"But we plan to help return as much of the money as we possibly can," Charlie said.

I nodded.

"Please, I prefer to be called Charlie," she said.

"If Charlie," Sam said, patting her arm, "and Kerry are able to help return some of the millions, then I'll do everything I can to make sure they don't face any criminal charges. I'll also speak to the DEA about your situation."

"Can you do that?" J.T. asked. "Return most of the money?"

"Yes," Kerry said, "Charlie took care of the finances for the 'Chosen.' She knows exactly where every penny of the money is stashed away."

"The Reverend made millions of dollars financing the El Bajio Drug Cartel," Charlie said.

"Is the money in U.S. banks?" Sam asked.

"Yes," Charlie said.

"All we'll have to do is get a couple of court orders," Sam interjected, "and figure out who the money goes to and how much. I'll get my staff on it as soon as I get back to Washington."

"I want to know something, Kerry," Paula said. "How did you walk away from your life the way you did and not miss your parents and friends?"

Paula studied J.T.'s demeanor and then floated her eyes back to see how Kerry would respond to her question.

"It's complicated," he said. "I met this woman," pointing to Charlie. "She taught me how to love and, before I knew it, I was under her spell."

"It was my fault," Charlie said. "I was mesmerized by Reverend Jackson's teachings and Kerry bought in to it the same way I did."

"It wasn't entirely your fault, Charlie," Kerry said. "I was ripe for his message. It was like nothing I had ever heard before."

"Paula," Charlie said, "we fell in love. Haven't you ever been in love before?"

Paula glanced down and then in my direction trying to make eye contact. I ignored the attempt and kept my focus on Charlie.

"When did you realize Reverend Jackson wasn't as apostolic as he made himself out to be?" Paula said.

"About a year after the 'Chosen' relocated to San Miguel," Kerry said.

"All of a sudden making money became his..." Charlie paused and seemed embarrassed, "god instead of the Lord."

"Everything changed after that," Kerry added, "but we were too faithful to him to believe he had changed."

"In fact, he had become a drug dealer," I said.

"That bothered me very much," Kerry said, "and then there was talk about him becoming a murderer."

"He was," I said.

Kerry stared at me for a moment and then dropped his head.

"When Luke was born we tried to overlook the depravity and just concentrate on our beautiful son," Charlie said as tears filled her eyes.

Kerry continued the saga.

"It got a little better after that, or maybe we just tried to push the bad stuff out of our minds. But last year the visits from strange and ungodly men became more frequent and some of our brethren began to disappear."

"Were they the ones questioning what was going on?" J.T. asked.

Kerry and Charlie both nodded without saying anything.

"We'll spend a day or so at Carswell," Sam said to Kerry and Charlie, "debriefing you and the rest of the former 'Chosen' before we release you, so let's hold off any more questions until then."

Kerry stood up and got down on his knees in front of Charlie. She leaned forward and they hugged, crying in each other's arms.

Chapter Fifty-four

Jeb Glasscock was ecstatic when I called him from Carswell Air Force Base. He said he would break the news to Glenn Vogel and fly the Sheriff and Kerry's mom to Fort Worth in the morning. I told him nothing other than we found him in Mexico, safe and sound. The rest would be a surprise.

Paula interviewed Kerry and Charlie before departing for her network's affiliate in Dallas to begin working on her story. Shaggy mentioned something about a documentary called 'Mission de Allende' after the story ran its course. Sam, who we were calling Congressman again, began the process of debriefing the former 'Chosen' with a member of his staff. The entire cast of 'Mission de Allende' planned to meet at Joe. T. Garcia's Mexican Restaurant tomorrow, after the Vogel family was reunited and a press conference was held at the base. Major Benji Atchison drove J.T. and me to Panta's Gym where my Malibu was still parked.

Dad was sitting barefooted on the back porch cleaning his Smith and Wesson .38, when J.T. and I arrived at his house. The shirttail of his wrinkled dark brown shirt hung over the waist of an old pair of khaki trousers frayed around the cuffs. Both were stained with drops of fish blood from past trips to the lake. A rag he was using to wipe off excess lubricant hung over the armrest of the chair he was sitting in. His outfit was diametrically opposed to the way he was attired the last time I saw him.

"I take it you're not working today," I said.

"Official announcement is day after tomorrow," he said, without looking up. "Until then, Mayor said to lay low. So, I'm layin' low."

Dad finally looked up at us.

"Hi, J.T.," he said.

"How ya doin', Emmett?"

"That should be *my* question," Dad said with a smirk on his face. "Panta called me the other day and said the Air Force showed up at his gym and took Pat away in a government vehicle."

"They sure did," J.T. said, chuckling.

"Then, Ernie calls me and tells me *you* show up outside his place and three Air Force uniforms wrestle you to the ground and take you away in handcuffs."

J.T. and I glanced at each other, amused by how much fun Dad was having teasing us.

"Then my son disappears for two days without giving me a call like he was on some secret government mission."

"Actually, Dad, we were."

We told Dad the entire story from beginning to end.

"You cracked your first case," Dad said with pride. "Now what are your plans?"

"Decide whether to set my office up here in Fort Worth, or accept Jeb's offer to set it up in Brownwood."

Dad went back to cleaning his gun. J.T. sat down in a lawn chair next to Dad and I leaned my backside against the railing of the back porch.

Dad made eye contact with me and said, "Made a decision?"

"Yes," I said.

J.T. studied my face trying to determine what the answer would be. He leaned forward with his elbows on his knees and his fingers interlaced.

"I'm going to begin looking for a place to live first thing in the morning and set up my office at the Glasscock Communications Center."

J.T. dropped his head in disappointment.

"Well, you know," he said. "That'll put me out of the game. Especially, since we've found Kerry."

"You have to do what you have to do," I said.

"Kerry's going to need me, Pat."

I nodded.

"You can do this on your own," Dad said. "We've talked about this already."

I nodded my head in agreement.

"Damn," J.T. said. "I was hoping you were leaning toward Brownwood. We've been having one hell of a good time."

That we have.

Dad was content laying low until the press conference on Friday officially announcing his appointment as the new Chief of Police. I dropped J.T. off in front of Ernie's Bar and Grill, where his late model Monte Carlo was parked. Three parking tickets flapped in the wind, held in place by the windshield wipers. J.T. said he was going to talk to Dad about fixing the tickets. He got in his car and drove to Carswell Air Force Base to spend the evening in the company of Kerry and Charlie. I pulled into the parking garage of the Glasscock Communications Center and took the elevator upstairs. Dottie sat behind her desk greeting me with a smile.

"We heard you got your man," she said, pleased with her quip.

Standing in front of her desk, I said, "Dottie, I want you to help me find a place to live."

"Good," she said. "That means you'll be coming back to us."

"Yes it does, but not the way you might expect."

Dottie tilted her head slightly and thought about what I possibly meant.

"I also want you to help me hire a secretary," I said. "Would it be possible for you to have three candidates for the job in here by Monday?"

"They'll be here first thing Monday morning," Dottie said.

"I'd like for them to have a law enforcement background."

"That can be arranged, as well," Dottie said. "Is that all?"

"No," I said, "I'd like my new offices down the hall furnished by Monday, too."

I turned around to leave.

"Is there anything else?"

"Tell, Wynn," I said, walking toward the elevator, "that I'm not interested in his offer."

"What are you going to do then?"

"I'm going to become a cop."

"What do you mean, Pat?"

I pushed the down button on the elevator and turned around to look at Dottie, who was now standing up behind her desk.

"Private," I said.

"You mean a private investigator?"

"Exactly," I said.

Chapter Fifty-five

Ernie stood in front of me behind the bar listening intently to the story of 'Mission de Allende' and how J.T. and I solved the mystery surrounding Kerry Vogel's disappearance.

"Is he…like…," Ernie made a circling motion with his right hand at the side of his head, "crazy?"

"No, they have been out of touch with society for quite some time, but they both seem to have come out of the experience in good shape. I really believe they've got their heads screwed on pretty straight…considering."

"Sometimes repressed emotions have a way of popping their ugly heads back up years later," Ernie analyzed.

His words hovered in the air as I ran Vietnam and Brett Tucker's murder around in my head.

"Will they face any charges?"

"Kerry hasn't broken a law in either country, as far as I know."

"What about the wife…what's her name?"

"Charlie," I said. "It's short for Charlene, but she prefers to be called Charlie."

Mammoth Mike placed a Heineken draught on a napkin in front of me and made his way to the end of the bar, where he took the drink orders for a couple that had just sat down.

I took a pull off the beer and said, "She could be facing some trouble in Houston. We're not sure exactly how involved she was, other than the fact she kept the books."

Ernie looked at his watch.

"The news will be coming on in a few minutes," he said. "I'll change all the TV's to Channel 8 and turn up the volume."

Harry Reasoner introduced Paula Conn a few minutes into the evening newscast. Shaggy had filmed her standup at Carswell with Jeb's Learjet in the background.

"United States Congressman Sam McCullough led a team of volunteers into Central Mexico earlier this week to rescue eight of his Houston area constituents being held against their will by the Reverend Malachi Jackson, the head of a religious cult known as the Church of the Chosen."

After Paula's lead-in, Shaggy had edited the film in a photomontage fashion, showing clips of Sam at several stages of the mission and a quick glimpse of the Rev from an old photograph.

"As seen in this exclusive film," Paula said, "Congressman McCullough is helping those held captive into a boat during the daring escape and rescue."

Shaggy was dead-on with his camera work as he captured the desperation on the faces of the 'Chosen' scrambling into the river. The screams for help from the men and women climbing into the barge added tremendous drama to Paula's journalism. The film cut away to a shot of J.T. coolly inventorying the scene to make sure everybody was onboard as he trimmed the motors back into the water and sped away from the river's edge.

"The rescue of Congressman McCullough's constituents was aided by a retired CIA operative identified only by his first name of Buck, and private investigator, Pat Cassidy, who was in Mexico to track down a missing person, also a member of the 'Chosen.' They provided cover-fire that allowed the rescue party to escape unharmed."

Shaggy spliced in a clip of Buck and me together sometime prior to the actual rescue. Then, he used the extent of the zoom on his camera to catch Paula briefly standing up from behind the rocks. Apparently, that was the moment just before I yanked her down on top of me.

"During an exchange of gunfire," Paula continued, "the Reverend Jackson, was mortally wounded. Congressman McCullough commented on the success of the mission."

The picture segued to Paula standing alongside Sam on the tarmac at Carswell Air Force Base.

"The mission was a great success," Sam said.

Shaggy zoomed in the wide shot to a facial close up of the Congressman.

"We are heartbroken about the casualties that resulted in this rescue mission. We *were* able to rescue our Houston area constituents without any of them being injured. Within twenty-four hours these people will be back home with their loved ones."

The story concluded with Paula standing in front of the Learjet again, saying, "This is Paula Conn, ABC News, on the tarmac of Carswell Air Force Base in Fort Worth, Texas."

When the picture on the TV set returned to Harry Reasoner, Ernie said, "Next time…will you try to get in a mention of your old hang out here?"

Chapter Fifty-six

"Pat Cassidy," Mammoth Mike said over the noise of the crowded bar. "You're my hero."

"Along with anyone else who drinks a lot," I said.

"Awww…Pat," he said. "You know better than that. Besides you're good for business."

"O.K., serve me up another beer and a shot of tequila."

"Sure thing, buddy, after all, you know I'm your favorite bartender."

Mike was a tall man with bulky muscles that were easily visible through a white short sleeve shirt. His long blonde hair was parted down the middle and reached his shoulders. Mike's pitted face was unshaven and the hair in his beard and eyebrows was darker than the hair on his head.

"Don't know of a more favorite one," I said. "Especially after you deliver me round two."

The empty glass in front of me made a high pitched ding when I flicked it with my index finger. Mike smiled, and then pointed with his eyes at the man standing behind me.

"Mr. Cassidy," the man said.

Without turning around, I said, "He's wearing a suit isn't he, Mike?"

Mike nodded with playful eyes.

The man sat down on the barstool next to me. Spinning my barstool in his direction, I recognized Congressman McCullough's staff member who had been helping him debrief the former 'Chosen' earlier in the day.

"You're Hank, right?" I said.

He nodded.

Mike put a fresh beer and tequila shot in front of me. I sucked on the lime, then licked the salt around the brim of the shot glass, and swallowed the Jose Cuervo.

"Want a beer?" I said.

Hank shook his head as I chased away the sting of the tequila with a swig of beer.

"Congressman McCullough would like to talk to you."

I scanned the bar looking for him.

"Where is he?" I asked.

"He would like to talk to you in private," Hank said.

"Take me to your leader."

Hank squinted at me disapproving of the sarcasm, and walked toward the front door. Putting down the glass of Heineken, I followed him. Once outside, Hank pointed toward a black limousine across the street with Major Benji Atchison leaning against the back fender.

"Pat," he said, as I walked up to the limo.

"Major," I said, giving him a wave that resembled a distant salute.

The Major opened up the back door.

"Get in," Congressman McCullough said, sitting on the opposite side of the backseat.

As I slid in next to him, the Major closed the door behind me. The Congressman handed me a briefcase.

"What's this?" I said.

"Payment for services rendered."

"Congressman," I said.

"Pat," he said, "please, call me Sam."

"I thought you wanted…"

"Forget about that. That was for the others…not you. I want you to call me Sam."

I nodded and opened the briefcase. It was full of money.

"How much?" I asked.

"A hundred thousand," Sam said.

I closed the briefcase and handed it back to him.

"This would be for what?" I said.

"I asked you to kill the Reverend Jackson," Sam said, handing the briefcase back to me.

I shook my head and he put it back on his lap.

"I shot him because he killed an innocent member of the 'Chosen' and was about to kill another one."

Sam unsnapped the briefcase and looked at the money.

"This is a lot of money, Pat."

I nodded.

"You could put this money in the bank and never have to work again the rest of your life."

"Where did you get the money?"

"It's just a small portion of the money I was planning on using to buy off Reverend Jackson."

I nodded again.

"Give me a pen," I said.

Sam reached inside his suit coat and pulled out a pen and handed it to me.

"Got something to write on?"

He pulled a small spiral notepad out of his inside pocket and tore out a page. I wrote Buddy Connor's name and address on the piece of paper.

"Deliver the money to this address and tell them it is compliments of Uncle Sam."

Chapter Fifty-seven

The next day it was windy and cloudy as I drove to Carswell for Sam's scheduled press conference. Howard Teaff, the WFTW meteorologist, talked on the radio about a mass of unstable cold air moving into West Texas.

"We'll see the effects of this front late tomorrow and on into Saturday," Howard said, "with an increased chance of thunderstorms that could possibly spawn a tornado or two here in the Metroplex."

The Military Policeman at the front gate had to hold down the sign-in sheet on his clipboard to keep it from flapping in the howling wind from the west. The blue name tag on his stiffly starched olive drab uniform had the name Jackson written in white letters. A common name, but the late Reverend Jackson came to mind. The MP's white helmet had a blue and silver sergeants' insignia on it and he wore a black arm band with MP scripted in large white letters.

"Have a good day, Mr. Cassidy," Sergeant Jackson said after looking at my signature.

I had dressed appropriately for the occasion and the weather. The cold wind tousled my once neatly combed hair as I stood alongside Sam and J.T. on the tarmac waiting for Jeb's Learjet to land. My brown leather jacket was zipped up over a yellow long sleeve buttoned down shirt and the holstered Browning. My khakis were starched and went well with the tan ostrich skin Tony Lama boots. J.T.'s rugged brown leather jacket was worn and faded and he wore it with a white silk t-shirt, blue jeans, and brown Justin Ropers. He stood bareheaded facing the wind with his jacket unzipped making his shoulder strap visible. Sam was dressed like you would expect a United States Congressman to dress. A gray Donegal tweed hat kept his head warm and a charcoal cashmere overcoat did the same for the rest of him.

"You need a haircut, Cassidy," J.T. said.

"It's on the list," I said.

Jeb's Learjet landed and taxied to within a few feet of us. A short while later Jeb, Sheriff Vogel, and his wife emerged from the plane.

Sam turned on the charm as Jeb approached. *Obviously he was one of Sam's biggest contributors.*

"Mr. Glasscock," Sam said, brandishing his patented politician's smile.

"Congressman," Jeb said, shaking his hand.

"Call me, Sam."

Jeb flashed his *aw shucks* smile and nodded. It was a disarming smile intended to put people at ease.

"Pat," he said. "J.T."

He shook hands with us.

"Great job you boys did." Turning to Sam, Jeb said, "Call me Jeb. Mr. Glasscock was my daddy's name."

Sam grinned with the invitation.

The Sheriff and his wife walked up and, without saying a word, Mrs. Vogel hugged J.T.

"How is he?" Mrs. Vogel asked.

"Kerry is great," J.T. said with enthusiasm.

"This must be Pat," she said.

I extended my hand.

"It's very nice to meet you, Mrs. Vogel."

"Come here and let me hug you, too." After the hug, she said, "Thank you for bringing my baby home."

Boy is she ever going to be surprised.

"Pat and J.T.," Sheriff Vogel said. "I don't know how to…"

"It's O.K., Sheriff," J.T. said. "We're all happy he's comin' home."

Major Atchison and Buck stood by to drive us to a nearby hanger where the press conference was to take place. The Major drove Sam, Jeb, Sheriff Vogel, and his wife to the hanger in the limousine and Buck drove J.T. and me to the location in a Jeep. Several television and radio news vehicles were parked in front of the hanger when we arrived. Inside, a makeshift stage had been erected in the middle of the structure that was normally the home of a B-52 bomber. The media took a position off to the left of the stage where TV cameras sat on tripods, radio newsmen carried tape recorders, and newspaper reporters wrote in their notebooks. Chairs, aligned in straight rows, were placed in front of the stage to accommodate the families that had made it to Fort Worth to welcome home the former members of the Church of the Chosen.

Kerry Vogel walked across the hanger toward his parents. At first I didn't recognize him. He had gotten a haircut, shaved his beard, and had traded his white religious cult garb for a new blue suit with a white shirt and red tie. He looked like the All-American boy that he once was. Paula and Shaggy trailed behind him. Shaggy was filming the impending reunion of the Vogels. Probably for the 'Mission de Allende' documentary Paula was planning.

"Mom...Dad!" Kerry shouted from across the hanger.

The Vogels recognized his voice and turned in his direction. Mrs. Vogel ran to Kerry with the Sheriff right behind her. They hugged and cried in each other's arms for a long time. We could see Charlie making her way through the crowd of families having their own individual reunions. Sam, J.T., and I all felt our collective hearts skip a beat the moment she stepped out into the open.

"She's even more beautiful," J.T. said with astonishment.

"The body of a goddess," Sam said with his mouth halfway open.

Charlie was dressed in a sultry gloss-black wrapped dress with long sleeves and a calf-length skirt with simple, but attractive spiked heels. Her long blonde hair was cut in an up-to-date shag and her makeup was captivating.

"Daddy…Daddy," Luke said, pulling away from his mother's grasp and running toward the Vogels.

Luke ran up to Kerry and grabbed him around his legs. We were too far away to hear what was being said, but Kerry spoke to his parents while he rubbed the top of Luke's head. By the time Charlie walked up to them, Mrs. Vogel had raised both of her hands to the side of her face overwhelmed by the news. A few seconds later, she fainted.

Chapter Fifty-eight

Mrs. Vogel was revived by a Houston doctor who was on hand to greet his cousin, Walter L. Davis. He said she would be fine, so everyone breathed a sigh of relief. Come to find out it was Charlie who had smuggled the letter out of the compound Mr. Davis wrote to Sam. The throng of people gathered for the press conference began to make their way to the seating area and up onto the stage. Shaggy had situated his camera in the middle of the aisle separating the two seating sections facing the stage. Paula and I stood behind the seating area watching Shaggy go about his business and the activity of people milling around on stage.

"They're not very happy with you right now," I said, motioning toward the media that was roped off and kept in check by a couple of MPs.

Paula peered at them for a moment.

"They didn't put their ass on the line like we did," she said. "If they had, they would be front and center like me. Besides, when I air 'Mission de Allende' they'll say I knew her when…"

"You really are putting this into a documentary?" I said.

"Next month," Paula said. "The network has given me clearance to air it during the May sweeps."

"Ratings," I said.

"That's what it's all about, my sweet."

Sam and his staffer, Hank, placed everyone on stage as if they were choreographing a Broadway show. Buck lingered on the edge of the stage, ever watchful of the crowd. J.T flanked the other side of the stage talking to Kerry and Charlie. The Vogels took a seat with their new found grandson and Jeb.

"You know we have some unfinished business, Mr. Cassidy," Paula said.

I looked at her and winked. Paula gave me a seductive smile. It was the second time today my heart had skipped a beat.

"It'll have to wait, though," she said. "Shaggy and I have been ordered back to New York."

I nodded with disappointment.

"It'll happen, Pat. Just keep that in mind."

Hank was at the microphone centered at the front of the stage. He spoke into the mic. "Testing…one…two…three…four."

He turned around and said something to Sam. After their short conversation, Hank returned to the microphone and Sam motioned me up to the stage.

"See ya later," I said to Paula and made my way next to J.T.

Hank spoke into the microphone.

"Ladies and gentlemen," he said, "I present to you a true American hero…United States Congressman…Sam McCullough."

The crowd warmly applauded. Kerry and Charlie stood on each side of Sam with his constituents lined up behind him ready for introduction. I was scanning the crowd, when I noticed two men stand up and nonchalantly walk up the aisle past Shaggy.

"Hey," Shaggy said as they passed by him, "you're in the way."

My first impression was they looked like ushers getting ready to take up the collection plate at church. Walking side by side, the men approached the stage. Suddenly, they pulled guns out from underneath their suit coats.

Buck shouted as he pulled out his Beretta, "Congressman! Get down!"

J.T. and I pulled our weapons as Sam raised his head to see the men walking toward him. The black man on the right raised his semiautomatic and took aim at Sam.

"No!" Kerry said, jumping in front of the Congressman.

Kerry was flatfooted with his arms outstretched in full frontal view of Sam when the assassin shot him in the midsection. He doubled over and crumpled to the stage floor. Screams echoed loudly through the hanger as the crowd ducked into the aisles. The second assassin, a short, thick Hispanic, took aim and the screams were overpowered by the explosion of gunfire. Buck, J.T., and I all opened fire at the same time, killing the two men before they could get off another shot.

Chapter Fifty-nine

"I suppose we were stupid to believe the El Bajio Cartel wouldn't try get back at us for killing the Rev," J.T. said.

"We're not stupid," I said. "A simple miscalculation is all it was. They're oh for four now. I don't think they'll be coming back. Sam said he would sick the DEA on them."

The Vogels, Charlie, and Jeb stood in the waiting room at Harris Methodist Hospital talking to a doctor who had just come out of the emergency operating room. J.T. and I were in the hallway watching them through the open door. There was good news as the Sheriff, Mrs. Vogel, and Charlie reacted to Kerry's prognosis. Jeb walked out of the waiting room to inform us.

"He's gonna be O.K.," he said.

"Thank God. I'm going in to be with them," J.T. said. He made his way into the waiting room.

"The bullet missed his vital organs," Jeb said.

"Kerry is a lucky man," I said.

Jeb nodded.

"It'd be a cryin' shame for him to die now after you found him and brought'em back after all these years."

"It would be a crying shame for his beautiful wife and son."

"Yep, Kerry's a fortunate man in more ways than one."

Out of Touch

In the waiting room, J.T. embraced Mrs. Vogel and shook the Sheriff's hand. He then put his arm around Charlie.

"You *are* comin' to Brownwood like I want you to, aren't you?" Jeb said.

I shook my head.

"It's been awhile since I've faced life and death situations. Seein' Kerry shot like that makes me realize how fragile life is."

"Yep," I said.

"Pat, you know I think of you as the son I never had don't you?"

"Yes I do, Jeb."

"Hell…I thought you and Kelly might even hit off."

"She's gotta a lot of growing up to do," I said.

Jeb nodded and lowered his head.

"Anyway," Jeb said, looking up at me, "I'm not that sentimental, but I was really lookin' forward to havin' ya in Brownwood."

"It's not going to happen, Jeb."

Jeb was disappointed.

"What you've done here is pretty special," he said. "I don't know of anyone else who could have pulled this off."

"Couldn't have done it without you," I said.

"May be the case, son, but it reinforces my belief in you."

"What belief is that?"

"That you'll get it done, no matter what job I hand you."

The doctor in blue scrubs came out of the waiting room greeting us with a smile veiled with exhaustion as she made her way back to the emergency room.

"When this is all over," Jeb said, "I want'cha to take a couple of weeks off. You've gotta be exhausted."

"I can't, Jeb. I've got a lot to do to get my office set up."

"Well, get it done and then take some time off. You're gonna need the rest. I've got somethin' goin' on with my football team that needs to be takin' care of before the start of next season."

"What's up?" I said.

"Somethin's goin' on with one of my bonus babies," Jeb said. "But don't worry about it right now. You've gotta enough on your mind."

The elevator a few feet away from us dinged as the door opened. Sam and Buck stepped into the hallway and made their way toward us.

"How is he?" Sam said.

Jeb told him.

"That young man saved my life," Sam said.

"He sure in the hell did," Jeb said.

"I've got to have him on my team."

"What team is that?" I asked.

"The team that's going to help me get elected President in four years," Sam said.

"I suppose you'll be wantin' my help?" Jeb said.

"As always," Sam said with raised eyebrows and a grin.

Geez. Here we go again.

Chapter Sixty

Friday morning I got up and drank a cup of coffee at Dad's kitchen table. I had the urge to hit something, so I stuffed my workout clothes in a gym bag and headed for Panta's Gym. Upon arrival I found him underneath his '57 GMC pickup truck.

"Why don't you trade in that old bucket of bolts?" I said, looking down at his feet sticking out from under the chassis.

Panta rolled out from under the truck on a mechanic's sled.

"I was thinking the same thing about that piece of shit you drive," he said.

"I challenge you to find another car that can out perform my SS."

"Good point," he said, getting up off the sled.

Panta picked up the sled and put it in the back of the truck upside down so it wouldn't roll around in the bed. He put two-bits in the parking meter and then walked to the front door of the gym and pulled out his keys.

"You were on TV again this morning," Panta said, glancing over his shoulder as he maneuvered the key into the lock.

"Hum," I said.

"So was your dad."

"Today is his big day," I said. "Emmett Cassidy, Chief of Police. It has a nice ring to it."

A gust of wind entered the gym with us as Panta unlocked the door. The force of the gust pushed the door out of Panta's grasp and slammed it against the wall.

"I think we're in for a storm later today," Panta said.

"*Riders on the Storm...*," I attempted to sing.

"That'd be you," Panta kidded. "Hey, I got an offer for you if you're interested."

"What's the offer?" I inquired.

"You're familiar with Perry Daniel aren't you?"

"Texas Heavyweight Champion out of Dallas. Ranked seventh in the world according to Ring Magazine...twenty-nine wins, five losses, twelve knockouts, and never been knocked down."

"Yeah...well, I guess you are familiar with him," Panta said.

"I used to be a sportscaster, Panta."

"Used to be?"

"Used to be," I said.

"What in the hell are you now?"

"As soon I get my license I'll officially be a private investigator."

"You're really gonna do this thing with Glasscock, aren't you?"

I nodded.

"Well…anyway, Perry wants to schedule a ten round exhibition fight sometime in June against a good amateur for charity. You interested?"

"What's the charity?"

"KICKSTART KIDS," he said.

"Chuck Norris' charity."

"Right…the kick boxing champion. Perry and his manager are puttin' together a card that'll have martial arts, kick boxing, and boxing. It's gonna be a pretty big deal. Course Perry's bout will be the main event."

"What's the date?"

"June third."

"That gives me about six weeks to get in shape," I said.

"Kid…you've never been out of shape."

Chapter Sixty-one

It was raining when I left Panta's Gym. The gnawing in my gut subsided somewhat with the lengthy workout and helped me get past some of the effects of jetlag. Panta would now be involved in every aspect of my conditioning between now and the June exhibition bout with Perry Daniel. The idea of getting back into the ring for a real boxing match sounded like fun.

The press conference to announce Dad as the new Fort Worth Chief of Police was scheduled for eleven in the morning at Will Rogers Auditorium. Mayor Castleberry wanted it over in time for lunch. The Mayor possessed a huge appetite and his large physique displayed the results, but he was an honest politician, and now his 'Top Cop' would also be honest.

The rain had stopped by the time I reached Dad's house. When I got out the car distant thunder rumbled through the warm air. It would rain off and on all day according to the forecast. Dad asked me to wear a suit and tie for the press conference. So, after getting cleaned up, I got out my one and only suit, removed the dry cleaners' plastic covering, and then searched through the dresser drawer for my one and only tie. The tan suit looked pretty good with a white shirt, tan boots, and a nine millimeter. Armed and dangerous, I was off to Will Rogers.

Detective Arthur Hagen sat next to me in the audience as Mayor Castleberry prepared to introduce Dad. He had worked with my father for several years. Arthur fidgeted nervously, which was his normal disposition.

"This is great, Pat," Arthur said, "your dad being Chief."

"He deserved this job a long time ago," I said.

"Yeah he did, yeah he did," Arthur said, as if he were in a hurry.

Dad sat in a chair behind the podium in a new official Fort Worth Chief of Police dark blue uniform. Sitting next to him was Bob O'Reilly, his former partner, and his choice as the new Assistant Chief of Police. They were flanked by his top ranking officers who were also mostly new appointments. Arthur, for obvious reasons, didn't make the list of promotions, but would continue to serve the department as a valuable and loyal detective.

"Here comes the Mayor," Arthur said, shifting in his seat.

Mayor Castleberry stepped up to the podium with Fort Worth's finest at his back. Old Glory, the Texas Flag, and the flag of the City of Fort Worth sat side by side on the right side of the stage in ascending, or descending order, depending on your point of view. Every available Fort Worth Police officer sat in the audience in dress blues. The Tarrant County Sheriff's Department was represented, so was the Texas Department of Public Safety, and a spattering of other police departments in the area. The media sat clustered together along the front row with television cameras scattered around the room and in the balcony behind us. Missing from the scene were Paula and Shaggy who flew out of DFW late last night. I thought of Paula in an intimate setting and the room became a little warmer.

"I want to thank all of you for coming today as we usher in a new era of law enforcement for the City of Fort Worth."

The Mayor received a spirited round of applause from the audience of mostly cops.

"Before we get started we'll have the presentation of the colors by the Color Guard from Carswell Air Force Base, the Reverend Homer G. Ritchie, Pastor of the First Baptist Church, will give our invocation, and the Pledge of Allegiance will be led by Former Texas Supreme Court Judge Abner V. McCall."

Dad gave a great speech in accepting the position and promised to run a department that would earn the respect of the community. He was inundated with requests for interviews from the media and well-wishers lined the auditorium waiting to talk to him. I got his attention and mouthed, "I'll catch you later." Dad nodded and was quickly led away by Bob O'Reilly for another TV interview.

The windshield wipers cleared the falling rain from my view as I drove back to Dad's. Howard Teaff, *The World's Greatest Weatherman*, as Brett used to call him, informed listeners of tornado warnings along a cold front that had stalled along a line stretching from Del Rio Texas to Ardmore, Oklahoma.

"Areas along this line will need to particularly be aware of the development of tornados over the next thirty-six to forty-eight hours. Counties southwest of Forth Worth currently under a tornado watch include Erath, Somervell, Comanche, Brown, McCullough and Menard."

Howard continued his weather report and the rain continued to fall even heavier as I turned onto Camp Bowie Boulevard. The sky darkened, thunder rolled, and lightning flashed. In order to take my mind off the weather, I made a mental list of things to do. *Call J.T. for an update on Kerry. Check. Call Dottie for an update on secretarial candidates. Check.* The mental list of things to do was too short, so I made a list of things I'd already done. *Track down the missing Kerry Vogel. Check. Make a decision on where to locate my office. Check. Inform Jeb about my decision. Check. Inform J.T. about my decision. Check. Inform Dad about my decision. Check. Inform Claire about... Damn...I knew I forgot something.*

Chapter Sixty-two

Claire's phone rang a dozen times unanswered, before I finally hung up. After thinking about it I was glad she didn't answer. I owed it to her to break the news in person. J.T. told me Kerry was recovering well and would remain hospitalized for several days. His plans were to remain with him until he was well enough to be released. It being Good Friday, Dottie had the day off, so I reached her at home. She was having difficulty finding qualified secretarial candidates on such short notice. It would be midweek before she could round them up. I watched the heavy rain from the backdoor cascade over the edge of the roof. It fell in sheets and in varying waves of intensity, reverberating loudly off the aluminum canopy over the patio. Thunder repeatedly rattled the windows and cracks of lightning amplified the severity of the storm. Something was telling me to clear the air with Claire and to do it today. Despite the threatening weather, I traded in my dress up clothes for a windbreaker, t-shirt, jeans, and tennis shoes, packed an overnight bag, and headed for Brownwood.

The World's Greatest Weatherman greeted me when I turned on the car radio, "A flash flood warning is in effect for Tarrant County until two o'clock this afternoon."

Traffic was heavy and moved tortoise-like through the cloudburst and deep puddles that collected on the streets. A rear-ender restricted the flow onto the exchange at Camp Bowie and Benbrook. By the time I reached US Highway 377, the rain began to ease up. The cat-and-dog weather played cat-and-mouse with me all the way to Brownwood. The rain discouraged me from pulling over at a couple of pay phones. Instead, I drove to KBRW radio and parked directly in front of the entrance. Due to the weather and holiday, traffic was nonexistent at a little after four o'clock. The curtains in the control room picture window were pulled back and the face of Billy Miller popped up into view. Billy is an industrious high school kid who works most of the part-time hours at KBRW.

"I need to use the telephone," I said, standing in the control room doorway.

He was cueing up a record when he looked at me. "Sure thing, Pat, help yourself. How 'bout this weather today?"

Billy's voice projected epiglottal squeakiness across the airwaves and in person.

"Poured down on me most of the way," I said.

"You drove all the way from Fort Worth in this stuff?" Billy said. "It must be something really important to bring you down here in this kind of weather."

"It is," I said, as I walked across the hallway to the sales office to call Claire.

The phone rang for a long time without an answer. I let it ring a few more times, and then finally hung up.

"We're under a tornado warning," Billy yelled from the control room.

"Until when?" I yelled back.

"Seven o'clock tonight!"

Claire had to be somewhere and the person that would know would be her mother, Maggie. I looked up her number in the phone book and dialed it. She answered *her* phone right away.

"Maggie," I said.

"Yeah-essss?" she said.

"This is Pat."

"I suppose you're lookin' for Claire."

"I am."

"She's spendin' the weekend at my parent's old farmhouse," Maggie said.

"Would you mind giving me the phone number?"

"Not at all, but the farmhouse has never had a phone."

"What's she doing out there?" I asked.

"Why don't *you*...ask *her*...that question?"

Maggie gave me directions, so in the pouring down rain I drove south out of town on the Brady Highway. A short time later the rain stopped, and as I turned right on County Road 201, the sun strangely began to peek through the black clouds on the western horizon. I followed the road through Dalzell until it narrowed into a driveway where Claire's car was parked in front of a small sandstone farmhouse with a red tin roof. In the distance stood a broken-down old barn and a windmill that was changing directions with the shifting winds. The sunlight escaping through the storm clouds reflected off the surface of a silver butane tank. The Mesquite Trees took on different shades of greens and browns with the unusual mixture of light and darkness. Nearby, a storm cellar loomed like a fortress, undaunted by the threatening sky. On the front porch I heard the sound of a radio coming from inside. I knocked on the door several times. Each time the knocks became louder.

"Claire," I said. "I need to talk to you."

I waited.

Claire," I said a little louder.

The door slowly creaked open.

Chapter Sixty-three

Claire was halfway cloaked behind a front door painted sandy brown to naturally blend with the sandstone. She was in all denim; a short sleeve top with an embroidered playground scene above the right pocket and her shirttail hung over a faded pair of Levi's. She had on a pair of Italian clog sandals with woven buckles.

"I have to say I'm surprised to see you," Claire's eyes glared through the screen door.

"Can I come in?"

"Well, since you're here," she said, unlatching the screen.

I wiped my feet on the doormat and stepped inside the living room with stained pine-paneled walls and decorated with Early American furniture. A braided oval rug covered the middle of the hardwood floor and a mission style chair with pecan arms and legs rested in the corner of the room with a reading lamp turned on above it. Claire apparently had been spending a lot of time in the chair reading. A stack of books sat on the floor nearby.

"I wanted to tell you in person…," I said, when she cut me off.

"Tell me what, Pat," Claire snapped, "that you ran off to Mexico with Paula? I already know that. I also know that there's no way I can compete with someone like her."

"That's not how it is, Claire. I just needed to tell you about my decision to stay in Ft. Worth."

"Whether I'm competing with Paula or Fort Worth doesn't really matter. What matters is that I'm not important enough to you to make you want to stay. I don't really want to talk about this anymore. I wish you'd just leave."

Claire walked back toward the door and made a sweeping motion with her arm.

"I want to be clear with you, Claire. I wish you'd hear me out."

"If you're not going to leave," she said with an icy stare, "then I will."

"I'm not leaving until we resolve this," I said.

Claire pushed open the screen door and bolted out of the house.

I sat down on the sofa waiting for her to come back. Billy Miller interrupted the song playing on the radio for an emergency weather report.

"The National Weather Service in Fort Worth reports several tornados on the ground in the area northwest of Brady and moving to the northeast at fifteen to twenty miles per hour. That would have the tornados moving directly toward Brownwood."

The screen door flew open and then slammed shut. I sprinted to the front porch searching for Claire. She was nowhere in sight. The sky was black in every direction and the air became perfectly still. Stepping off the front porch, I noticed the open barn door. Figuring that was where Claire had gone, I rushed toward the barn when the black menacing clouds above spiraled downward and formed a funnel cloud. A tornado began to chew up a grove of Mesquites on a distant foothill out beyond the barn as a powerful gust of wind hit me full force almost knocking me down. Then, as if someone had opened a floodgate from above, a cold torrential rain began to fall. Through the wind and rain I trudged forward as the funnel cloud zigged and zagged in the direction of the barn. Just as I reached the structure, the swirling winds ripped the door off its hinges. Claire was curled up in the corner of a stall with her hands over her head by the time I made it inside.

"Claire," I shouted. "We've got to get to the storm cellar!"

She ran toward me as the backside of the barn was pulled away by the storm.

"Grab my hand," I shouted, hanging onto a beam in the middle of the collapsing structure.

Claire reached out and clasped both of her hands around my outstretched right arm. She was sucked off her feet by the ferocity of the wind and began to slide away from me. The roof began to peel away in sections. Suddenly, her body lifted upward and then slammed hard to the ground, knocking her unconscious. I picked Claire up in my arms and carried her limp body toward the storm cellar as the howling wind collapsed the barn behind us. Realizing we weren't going to make it, I laid Claire down in a ditch and threw my body on top of her.

Chapter Sixty-four

"You were lucky to escape with your life," Jeb said in the parking lot of the Brownwood Regional Hospital. "We all were. The tornados skirted to the south and missed the rest of the area."

It was almost midnight and the cold front that had brought the violent weather earlier in the day had moved on, leaving in its wake a starry night.

"How's Claire?" Jeb asked.

"She has a pretty good bump on her head," I said. "Maggie said the doctors will release her first thing in the morning."

"Chalk up another one for Pat Cassidy," Jeb said.

"The funnel cloud flattened the barn then disappeared into the clouds."

"If you hadn't been there, Claire would've been killed."

"If I hadn't been there, she wouldn't have been in the barn."

"You don't have any way of knowin' that for a fact do ya?"

"Guess not," I said. "Thanks for checking on us."

Jeb shook my hand and drove back to the ranch.

Maggie stopped me on the way back into the hospital.

"Claire's sleeping," she said.

"I'd like to see her before I head back to Fort Worth."

"You're headed back at this late hour?" Maggie said, surprised.

"Don't have a reason to stick around here."

"Claire told me she is indebted to you for saving her life."

I nodded.

"She doesn't want to see you right now." Maggie's eyes were sincere. "Claire also said nothing else needs to be discussed between you two."

"Then I guess tell Claire I'll see her around."

Without saying another word I walked to the Malibu and began the long drive back to Fort Worth. It was three in the morning when I pulled into Dad's driveway and parked behind his new police unit. Making my way into the house as quietly as possible, I got a beer out of the refrigerator and sat down at the kitchen table. Dad came in wearing an undershirt and boxers and sat down on the other side of the table.

"Wanna tell me about your day?" Dad asked.

"Nope," I said. "Wanna tell me about yours?"

"Nope."

"I think I'm going away for awhile," I said and took a swig of the beer.

"Where to?"

"Don't know."

"How long?"

"A couple a days," I said. "Jeb told me to take a couple of weeks off but I can't see myself doing that with everything going on right now."

"Maybe you should," Dad said. "You've been burning the candle at both ends for the better part of two months. Two weeks away from everything could be just what the doctor ordered."

I nodded and drank some more of the beer.

"What's going on with Kerry? Is he going back to Brownwood when he gets out of the hospital?"

"J.T. told me earlier today…," I looked at the clock on the kitchen wall, "actually it was yesterday…that the Congressman was going to take them back to Washington with him. He is going to put them in charge of an outreach program he plans to finance with some of the Reverend Jackson's drug profits."

"That's not quite legal," Dad said with a raised brow.

"The Congressman is a very powerful politician."

Dad gestured with a tired movement of his head and left it alone.

"I suppose this is the best for them."

"You mean Kerry and Charlie?"

"Yeah."

"He can't go back to Brownwood," I said. "He'll always be the weird religious freak."

"But in Washington," Dad said, "he'll fit right in."

We laughed.

"Where does that leave J.T.?"

"He told me flat-out he's staying in Brownwood."

We were quiet for awhile. I heard the refrigerator compressor click on and begin to hum.

Then he said, "Pat, I've decided to sell the house."

This was the last thing I expected to hear from Dad sitting in his kitchen in the middle of the night. I took a long drink out of the bottle and finished the beer.

"Why?" I said.

"I haven't sold it before now because of sentimental reasons, but the time has come to move on."

"You're buying another house…or what?"

"I'm buying a new condominium in a high-rise near the downtown area. It has a state-of-the-art security system, underground parking garage, the works. I'll need the added security with my new position as Chief of Police."

"What about the lake house?" I asked.

"I'll never sell the lake house. It's where I go to recharge my inner battery."

"You have any other news to shock me with?"

"Oh, there is one other thing," Dad said. "It came in the mail yesterday, but with everything going on, I forgot to give it to you."

Dad got up and walked through the living room to his office. A minute later he came back and sat down, sliding a manila envelope across the table. It was addressed to me from the State of Texas.

"I made a call to Pat Spier at the Department of Public Safety," Dad said as I opened the envelope, "and he made a call to Secretary of State Mark White, and he was able to push your application through all the red tape."

Inside the envelope was a letter from the Secretary of State officially notifying me that I was a duly licensed and bonded private investigator in the State of Texas.

"Congratulations, son," Dad said. "You're officially a private dick."

Yippee!

Chapter Sixty-five

The view from the Tavern Room was breathtaking as the sun set behind the Berkshire foothills and melted into the water along the western shore of Lake Waramaug. I was enjoying a warm intimate fire with a cold Heineken at Hopkins Inn, a nineteenth century Victorian style country inn in Northwest Connecticut. This would be my home for the next two nights. Pondering over the items on the menu made me realize choosing an appetizer and entrée would be a difficult task. The *Clams Casino* and *Pate a la Maison* sounded like particularly tasty appetizers. I drank the remainder of my beer and looked around for Benny, the waiter.

"Another beer, sir?" he said as if he'd been standing behind me the entire time.

"Please," I said, and went back to studying the menu.

After a process of elimination, I had pretty well narrowed the entrée choice down to two selections. At this point I would probably order *Wiener Schnitzel* or *Veal Kidneys Dijionaise*, but I still wasn't certain.

"Here is your beer, Mr. Cassidy," Benny said.

"Are you ready to order?"

"Umm, not yet."

I flipped the menu over to the back where the desserts were located and systematically calculated which of them would taste better after any one of the combinations of appetizers and entrées I ended up ordering. Cheesecake Hopkins won out. Benny walked by my table with a tray of drinks in his hands.

"If you're ready to order I'll be right back."

"Thanks, Benny" I said, "but I think I'll read the paper before I order."

A book called *The Choir Boys* I picked up at the airport sat on top of the latest edition of Sports Illustrated Magazine and today's Hartford Courant. I slid the paper out from under the book and periodical, finding the sports page. It was great having time to relax and read through the box scores. Extenuating circumstances had denied me lately of one of my greatest joys in life.

"You sure know how to make it hard for a girl to say no."

I looked up at Paula standing on the other side of the table.

"Wow," I said, "some dress."

The peach mini dress fit snug along the curves of her body and advertised her firm sexy legs.

"This little ol' thang," Paula said, making a flipping motion with her hair and faking a southern accent. "Why, thank you, kind sir."

I stood up and pulled a chair out for her. As she sat down, I noticed the matching high heels.

"I see chivalry isn't dead," she said, still in character.

"You look so beautiful," I said.

"A girl can never hear *that* enough," Paula said, losing the accent. "I see you got a haircut. It looks nice…and is that a new jacket?"

"I received a nice bonus from Jeb for finding Kerry Vogel."

"Were you planning on doing a lot of reading?" Paula said, eyeing the book.

"Now that you're here I have other plans. I have to admit," I said, holding my hands up, "I wasn't sure you would come."

"You sent me red roses, you devil. How did you know they are my favorite?"

"I *am* a private investigator."

I pulled out my new license to show her.

"Pat, that's wonderful news!" she said with a scintillating smile.

Paula took the license out of my hand to get a closer look at it.

"Thanks," I said. "It usually takes three to four months, but Dad pulled a few strings."

"So, who told you I love red roses?" Paula said, handing the license back to me.

"Shaggy."

Benny interrupted us.

"Will you be having a guest for dinner?" he asked.

"Yes, I will. Paula, would you like a drink?"

"A glass of Riesling," Paula said, smiling at Benny, which really pleased Benny.

"How was the drive?" I said with a sneaky grin.

"Marvelous, thanks to you. You are such a stinker sending a chauffeur driven limousine to bring me here."

"Do you have any luggage?"

"Yes, but what I am wearing tonight is small enough to fit in my purse."

Paula patted the small clutch purse sitting on top of the table.

"When do you have to go back?"

Benny brought the glass of Riesling. Paula took a sip.

"Tomorrow's Easter." She hesitated, peering at me over the top of the wine glass. "Or, did you think of that as well?"

"What kind of man do you think I am?" I said, trying to sound innocent.

"I *know* what kind of man you are, Pat Cassidy."

"Is that good or bad?"

"We'll see."

Paula sipped her wine and I finished my beer. Benny barely let me put down the empty glass before he was standing next to the table.

"Would you like for me to bring you another beer, Mr. Cassidy?"

Paula and I were locked in an amorous stare.

"Benny, you got anything stronger than beer or wine?"

Benny apologized.

"That's too bad," I said with my eyes still latched on to Paula's.

"Yeah," finally breaking the eye contact, "another beer will be fine."

"Where were we?" Paula said, lifting her chin and fanning her face with the menu. "Is it getting hot in here or is it just me?"

I left that one alone. Paula stopped fanning and opened the menu.

"What's good to eat on the menu?"

"Everything," I said, staring at her.

Paula took her eyes off the menu and glanced up at me.

"Stop it," she said.

"Stop what?"

"You're staring at me."

"I can't help it," I said, giving her my cuddly, puppy dog face.

"Are you really hungry?" Paula said.

"No," I said.

"O.K., will you promise me breakfast in bed?"

"You have my word," I said.

"That's good enough for me."

On the Range

A Pat Cassidy Novel

Enjoy the following excerpt from Pat Cassidy's next adventure... coming soon

Chapter One

My new office suite in the Glasscock Communication Center in downtown Fort Worth was bustling with activity as I sat in an old office chair behind an even older desk donated by WFTW radio down the hall. The new office furniture we ordered was just now arriving, a man from the phone company I knew from high school was stringing wires through the ceiling for a multi-line phone system, and the air conditioning was on the blink on an unusually warm day in late April. To make matters worse, I didn't like any of the women I had interviewed for the secretarial job.

"Mr. Cassidy, where do you want this?" a man said, rolling a filing cabinet on a dolly through the front door.

I pointed toward my office door.

"There are two more," he said, rolling past me. "Where do you want *them*?"

"Put them against the wall behind me," I said, pointing over my shoulder with a thumb up.

"I liked the second one you interviewed," the phone man, Ray Deans said from a ladder pulling wires through an opening in the ceiling.

"You would, Ray, wouldn't you?" I smiled, looking up at him.

Ray already had nine years in with General Telephone Company. In high school he was known as the class clown.

"She had nice hooters and a great…"

"All right, already, Ray," I said, cutting him off. "She was a great looking woman, but there was something about her that annoyed me."

"Probably that nasal whiney voice," Ray said, impersonating her.

Over the next hour, the office began to take shape as the rest of the new furniture was brought in and Ray completed his ceiling work, putting the panels back in place.

"It's hot in here, Cassidy," Ray said.

"Well, if you'll get my phones hooked up I'll call someone to fix it."

"You need a secretary, man."

"What I *need* is a phone," I said.

"Workin' on it, workin' on it," Ray said. "Where's the main terminal for the building?"

"Ask Joe Bob, the Chief Engineer at the radio station. He can tell you."

Ray exited through the propped open glass front door freshly painted with the words:

PAT CASSIDY
PRIVATE INVESTIGATOR
GLASSCOCK INTERNATIONAL, INC.

Alone for the first time in awhile, I began rearranging furniture until a woman spoke to me with a raspy know-it-all tone of voice.

"Well, doesn't this place look like crap?"

In the doorway stood a sassy looking lady who had probably already seen her sixtieth birthday. She was barely five feet tall with salt and pepper hair framing a pair of brown eyes that gave me the impression she didn't miss a trick. Her petite frame was dressed in a red polyester suit with a white ruffled blouse. She wore black no nonsense pumps with a matching handbag.

"Can I help you?" I said.

"I don't know about that, darlin', but from the looks of things around here, I can probably help *you*."

I looked around the place.

"Yeah, somebody needs to," I said. "I'm Pat Cassidy."

"I know who you are, honey," she said matter-of-factly. "I'm Sally Anne Beck."

We shook hands.

"What can I do for you, Sally?"

"Well, for starters you can give me a job, since your *father* fired me this morning."

"Is that so?" I said, fighting back the urge to smile. "Why would he do something like that?"

"Seems your *father*," Sally said, "doesn't want me as his secretary. I've been secretary for the Chief of Police for twenty-five years. In that time I've seen three Chiefs come and go and I've always done my job quite well."

"He let you go without giving you any reason why?"

"Oh, no, honey," Sally said, "he gave me a reason, but not a good one. Chief Cassidy said he thought it would be better if he brought in his *own* gal. He said it would be best if we cut ties and go our separate ways."

"So he sent you to me?" I said.

"Yes."

Thanks, Dad.

"I am looking for a secretary."

"You're not going to be one of those men who dilly dallies around about making decisions are you? God knows I'm not getting any younger."

"I'll call my dad to verify everything you told me and if it checks out you can start in the morning."

Sally gazed around the office.

"I tell you what," Sally said, "you call your dad, and in the meantime, I'll go home and change into my dungarees and come back and get this place shipshape."

"I like that idea, Sally. Welcome aboard."

We shook hands to finalize the deal.

"I'll pick us up some lunch, Pat. We've got a lot of work to do. Oh, by the way, my friends call me Sal."

Ray walked in the door as Sal left, and with a rubberneck jerk of his head, said, "Who's that?"

"That, my friend Ray, is my new secretary."

Ray's happy-go-lucky expression turned to one of confusion.

"You hired her?" Ray said.

I nodded with a smirk on my face.

"Cassidy, Cassidy, Cassidy, didn't I teach you anything in high school?"

"You should have been here," I said. "You would've thought she had just hired me."

Great Book.
Finished 3/14/11
Started 2:30 P.M. 3/13/11   12:15 A.M.

About the Author

This is E.P. Garth's second Pat Cassidy novel. Garth is a former sportscaster, a fabulous cook, and teaches in Louisiana. He and his wife, Sue, live on Toledo Bend Lake where they can still see their beloved Texas from their deck.

To learn more about the author, visit www.epgarthlearn.com or become a fan of E.P. Garth on Facebook.

LaVergne, TN USA
31 January 2011
214606LV00003B/8/P